Praise for

"A Hollywood adventure that's truly out of this world!
Alien Superstar has it all . . . action, suspense,
and big laughs!"
—Jeff Kinney, author of the Diary of a Wimpy Kid series

"Henry Winkler and Lin Oliver keep us laughing while
slipping in a lesson for kids—accept everyone as they are,
even if they have suction cups for feet . . .
A super fun read."
—Jennifer Garner

"Out of this world . . . will resonate with any kid who
has felt like an outsider."
—*Booklist*

"A funny interstellar adventure that will have readers
watching the cosmos for the second book to arrive."
—*School Library Journal*

HOLLYWOOD VS. THE GALAXY

For Indya, Ace, Lulu, Jules, August, and the new grandbaby
who's on the way. You bring us joy, and I wish you peace
on Earth. And to Stacey, always.
—H.W.

For Noa Lenore Baker, my beloved granddaughter. As you
would say, "Here ya go!" With love from your Noni.
—L.O.

Cataloging-in-Publication Data has been applied for and may be obtained from the Library of
Congress.

ISBN 978-1-4197-4684-0

Printed and bound in U.S.A.
10 9 8 7 6 5 4 3 2 1

Amulet Books are available at special discounts when purchased in quantity for premiums and
promotions as well as fundraising or educational use. Special editions can also be created to
specification. For details, contact specialsales@abramsbooks.com or the address below.

Amulet Books® is a registered trademark of Harry N. Abrams, Inc.

ABRAMS The Art of Books
195 Broadway, New York, NY 10007
abramsbooks.com

PROLOGUE

Hey there, everyone. I didn't see you at first, but I'm glad you're there. It's me, Buddy Cheese Burger, but you can hold the cheese and just call me Buddy Burger. It's been a while since we've hung out together. I'm still here on Earth, still starring in a television show called *Oddball Academy*, still eating twelve to fifteen avocados a day, and still having some problems with my biological alteration. Which, by the way, I'm in the middle of now so give me a minute to see if I can get this under control.

I arrived at the studio this morning in my human form as Zane Tracy, and before I can go to rehearsal, I have to become my full alien self, since I play an alien on the show. My left side cooperated perfectly, but my right side is refusing to transform. What I am right now is half human, half alien. This is not a pretty sight, so I'm going to ask you to close your eyes. Oh, wait a minute, if you close your eyes, you won't be able to read.

Okay, here's the new plan. You stay where you are with your eyes open, and I'll just step behind the page until my transformation is complete.

Here I go. Can you see me?

If you could, you'd see that my right hand is really putting up a fight and my five human fingers are not wanting to become my seven spiny alien fingers. I can't blame them, because the human ones are much more attractive with their trimmed nails and fleshy knuckles. And my right knee is being even more stubborn. I am going to ground it if it doesn't hurry up and follow the rules. I have been trying to transform it for the last ten minutes and it simply refuses to be become alien. That's because the knees on my planet don't get much attention, but here on Earth, you humans give your knees a lot of respect. You have knobby knees, chapped knees, sprained knees, dirty knees, scraped knees. There are even creams for knees and special knee bandages. I can't blame my human knee for not wanting to give up all that attention and become just another ignored part of an ordinary alien leg.

Anyway, I'm going to have to concentrate if I want to make this biological alternation happen, so if you'll excuse me, I've got to get down to business. I'll be back with you in Chapter 3.

See you then.

1

Bright purple blood oozed from Citizen Cruel's fingers, all fourteen of them, and dripped into slippery puddles on the floor in front of her. Three weeks of trying to claw her way out of the cramped concrete cage that held her prisoner had taken its toll on her body. She hadn't slept during that time. Nights were spent trying to free herself. During the day, she submitted to the poking and prodding of the team of scientists studying her, lying there in a limp heap, pretending to be dead.

"Alien specimen number 34," she heard the humans in their white lab coats say. "Appears to be female. Seven feet three inches tall. Weighs 340 pounds. Suction cups on her feet. Cobalt-blue skin, purple blood, six rotating eyes."

"Those would sure come in handy for driving," one of the male scientists chuckled. "You wouldn't need a rearview mirror."

"Or a side mirror, for that matter," a female one chimed in.

Then they all laughed their snorty, condescending laughs.

"She smells like a three-day-old fish," a third scientist with long black hair and a long nose said, as she took a skin sample with a pair of tweezers.

She should talk! Citizen Cruel thought. *She smells worse than a pile of dead dung beetle bodies on my planet.*

"She certainly is one ugly alien, that's for sure," the male scientist said.

Their remarks made Citizen Cruel furious. What did they know of beauty, these ridiculous humans? She was, in her own humble opinion, one of the most beautiful examples of an a supremely fit alien from her red dwarf planet. Why else would she have been chosen by the Supreme Leader himself for the dangerous mission to come to Earth and capture Citizen Short Nose, the runaway child who had fled their planet?

At night, when the scientists had finished with their examinations and gone home to eat their nutritionally empty pizza pies with their little human families, Citizen Cruel would work on her escape plan. She had vowed to herself that no humans, even the ones at the hidden-away Center for Alien Studies, could keep her captive. She would set herself free.

When she was moved from the examining table into her concrete prison box each evening, she would scratch at the same spot on her cage wall with her long, pointed fingernails. She dug into the thick concrete until her fingertips bled purple, boring an ever-deepening hole that she hoped would be just big enough to slip one of her spiny fingers through. It was lucky that her fingernails grew at the rate of eight inches a day, so each night, she had a new set of sharp nails to pursue her labor. She was hoping to see a ray of light that would tell her she had broken through the concrete wall. Then she would pick the lock and release the heavy metal chain that kept the lid above her tightly sealed.

One particular night, exactly eighteen days after she had been brought to the Center for Alien Studies, Citizen Cruel had a breakthrough. Literally. She could feel the concrete in front of her give way, and small chunks begin to crumble. Despite the pain in her fingers, she pressed on, ignoring the purple blood that dripped from her hands. She dug faster, more urgently, like an injured animal clawing its way out of a trap. This was no time to give in to pain. This was the time to push forward until . . .

YES!

THERE IT WAS!

A thin beam of light streamed into the darkness of her cramped cement cage.

With her heart beating fast, Citizen Cruel slipped her finger through the hole. She groped around blindly until her fingernail finally struck the metal lock that was holding the heavy chain in place. Carefully, slowly, she inserted her fingernail into the lock and turned. Nothing. She pushed harder until she felt her nail start to splinter. She stopped suddenly, terrified that the nail would break off completely and jam the lock.

Stay calm, she thought to herself, taking a deep breath and filling her three lungs. *The Supreme Leader is counting on you.*

Proceeding with microscopic precision, she wiggled her nail ever so slightly . . . to the left and to the right . . . until she heard a click. It was the click of freedom.

Her six eyes spun with excitement, rotating around her head like they were on a speedway. Pushing herself onto her knees, her powerful back began to raise the lid above her. As she strained to stand up, she could feel the heavy chains loosen until at last they slid down the concrete walls like a ribbon coming off a present. When she heard the *thunk* of the metal links landing on the linoleum floor, she knew she had achieved her goal. She gathered her strength, rose to her full height, and raised her fists to the ceiling.

"Citizen Cruel is back," she said to no one but herself. "These humans will not contain me!"

Quickly, she searched the room and found her possessions laid out on the examining table. She strapped her holographic watch onto her wrist, pulled her spacesuit on over her head, and grabbed a length of metal chain that she could use as a weapon in case she met with human resistance.

Citizen Cruel pushed open the door and peered into the hall. It was the middle of the night, and the long, white hall was empty except for a sleeping guard slumped at a desk in front a door that said DO NOT ENTER: BIOHAZARD AREA. Holding her breath, Citizen Cruel crept silently by him. The suction cups on her feet made a popping sound as they lifted off the linoleum tiles, and the noise startled the guard awake. When he laid eyes on her, he reached for his walkie-talkie and opened his mouth to shout.

"Oh no you don't," she growled at him. "I have something else in mind for you."

She zoomed directly over to him and then disappeared into his body, never coming out the other side.

"What is going—" he started to say, but midsentence, his voice changed into the voice of Citizen Cruel.

"Oh, I forgot to mention, I'm a body snatcher," her voice said. "You're me now."

The guard, whose body was now occupied by Citizen Cruel, walked down the hall toward the building exit. At the door, he came face-to-face with Cecilia Nunez, another guard on her way into the building.

"Hi, Gordon," Cecilia said. "I'm here to start my shift. You going home?"

"Yeah." Citizen Cruel spoke from deep within the body of the guard. "I'm going home to have some of that doughy stuff with tomatoes and cheese."

"Why don't you just call it pizza, Gordon, like the rest of us do?" Cecilia said with a friendly grin.

"Why don't you mind your own business?" came the cruel reply.

"What's got into you, Gordon?" Cecilia said, shaking her head. "No need to be so nasty."

Without answering, Citizen Cruel pushed past Cecilia, nearly knocking her down.

"Nice seeing you too," Cecilia called out as the door slammed behind her.

It had been weeks since Citizen Cruel had been outside, and she blinked hard to adjust to the early-dawn light. She saw that she was in a compound of low-slung brick buildings surrounded by a chain-link fence with barbed wire at the top. There were no people moving about, and the only noise she heard was the rumbling of a garbage truck pulling up to a row of trash dumpsters.

That gave her an idea.

"Okay, Gordon, this is where we split up," she said out loud. "Thanks for the ride, but it looks like my next one is here."

Citizen Cruel left the guard's body the same way she entered—through his skin. She burst out of him, leaving the poor, confused man lying in a heap on the pavement. With a few mighty leaps worthy of a superhero, she bounded across the parking lot and flung herself at the garbage truck. Her suction cups grasped onto the side. Stretching her huge body to its full height, she pulled herself up and over the top of the truck. Unseen by the driver, she dropped into the back of the truck, already half filled with the morning's garbage.

Inside, the smell was overpowering. Citizen Cruel gagged as she inhaled the rotting fumes of eggshells and soggy newspapers mixed with coffee grounds and tuna fish cans.

Suddenly, she heard the engine rev and felt a lurch forward as the driver pulled the truck up to a row of dumpsters. He slid the forklift under the first dumpster and lifted it high in the air. Citizen Cruel looked up just in time to see a large load of garbage pouring down onto her face. The first load of garbage to hit her wasn't so bad, because it was mostly shredded paper from offices. But the next load from the second dumpster contained the garbage from bathrooms, which was considerably more stinky. As it hit her, her stomach did a somersault, and she felt like she was going to pass out from the smell.

Once again, her sense of duty overcame her personal pain. Ignoring her queasy stomach, Citizen Cruel pressed a button on her holographic watch. The screen lit up, casting a pale green glow inside the dark truck. The coffee grounds sparkled like fairy dust and even the paper towels from the lavatories took on an emerald hue.

"Emergency call for the Supreme Leader," Citizen Cruel barked into the microphone on her watch. She held up the device and pointed the intergalactic antennae in the direction of her home planet. "Come in, Supreme Leader."

All that came through was static.

The truck lurched again as it approached the next dumpster. Citizen Cruel leapt high into the air and grabbed hold of the rim of the hopper, hanging on with one hand and pointing her holographic watch at the sky with the other.

"Come in, Supreme Leader," she repeated. "It's a matter of great urgency."

Once again, all she received was static, followed by a dumpster load of leaves, cut grass, and leftover manure that had been used as fertilizer. Both the smell and the weight of the trash knocked her down, and she found herself lying back on the bed of garbage.

"I have no connection," she shouted into the microphone, wiping some manure out of eyeballs number two and six. "Alpha Centauri must be blocking our frequency. I need to readjust my angle."

Wasting no time, Citizen Cruel dove into a pile of cardboard boxes and piled them into a tower. She climbed up and perched herself on the top, pointing her watch's antennae in the direction of the red dwarf planet she called home.

"Supreme Leader, can you hear me now?" she hollered into her wrist.

Suddenly, the pale green light from her watch deepened in color and grew so bright that Citizen Cruel had to shield her eyes. The powerful beam streamed out of her watch and swirled into a glowing mist that pulsated directly in front of her until the outline of a face began to appear.

The face was speaking, but she couldn't tell who it was nor could she make out the words. Only one thing was clear.

The talking face was really, really angry.

2

A dust storm was raging on the red dwarf planet, but the Supreme Leader barely noticed the sand pelting the windows as he paced around Grandma Wrinkle's stark circular prison pod. There was only one thing on his mind—punishing Buddy Burger for his unforgivable act of rebellion.

"That grandson of yours must be returned from planet Earth and taught a lesson," he bellowed into Grandma Wrinkle's face, stomping his foot in childish anger.

"Go easy on the stomping," Grandma Wrinkle said. "You'll pop your suction cups."

"Will not," he shouted.

"Will too," she shouted back. "You've already demanded my grandson's return a thousand times."

"And yet, there he is on Earth, which I will not tolerate. He is setting a hideous example for all my other subjects. Every citizen here is forbidden to leave—except me, of course, when I vacation on planet CocoCerus."

"That's one of the many things wrong with your corrupt government." Grandma Wrinkle spat out her words, unafraid of this raging bully. "You relax by the side of a polar pool while your people are joyless under a blazing red sun."

"Enough from your mouth!" The Supreme Leader shouted at top volume, activating the voice amplifier that was embedded in his vocal cords.

"If you can pipe down for a moment, you'd notice that someone's calling you," Grandma Wrinkle said, pointing to the holographic watch he wore on his wrist. "Your entire arm is vibrating green."

"You don't have to tell me that. I am acutely aware of everything around me."

The Supreme Leader spun around in the tight space and bumped smack into the wall.

Grandma Wrinkle laughed. "And that is why I used to call you Clumsy when we were young, nine hundred years ago. A fitting nickname. You could trip over air."

"Watch your tongues. I don't want to hear your memories. Remember, you are my prisoner and whether you live or die is in my hands."

Grandma Wrinkle kept smiling. "Speaking of which, your hand is still vibrating green, Mr. I'm-acutely-aware-of-everything."

Shooting her a foul look, the Supreme Leader stepped out of the tiny prison pod and pressed the receiver button on his watch. Citizen Cruel's face rose out of the screen and formed a 3D-image floating before his eyes.

Grandma Wrinkle craned her neck so she could see.

"Oh no," she muttered. "Not her again."

"Cruel!" the Supreme Leader snarled when her face became clearly defined. "Where have you been, you inept failure! You are a disgrace to the Squadron! You have ignored my calls. You have not checked in daily as I require. You have single-handedly botched this entire mission."

"I can explain, sir," the hologram of Citizen Cruel said. "Three weeks ago, I was captured and taken to the Center for Alien Studies, where I have been locked away in a living tomb."

"Spare me the details of your inadequacy. I don't care what happened to you. I only care that the boy is brought to me. Where exactly are you now?"

"I am in a moving vehicle somewhere in Colorado."

"Colorado! What galaxy is that?"

Grandma Wrinkle let out a tired sigh.

"It's a beautiful state, Clumsy," she said. "In America. In the movies, people are always going there to ski and drink hot chocolate with marshmallows."

"Movies! Do not speak that word. You know they are forbidden."

"But Clumsy . . ."

"Stop calling me that!"

"I'm just asking you to remember . . . we used to have fun watching Earth movies, before you outlawed them. Remember how we laughed at *Hot Shots from Outer Space?* And held hands during *Kissy Kissy Face Face.*"

"Quiet! Movies are like music and art and books. They give people ideas. Dangerous ideas that my government is opposed to such as—"

Suddenly his voice was drowned out by a loud rumbling sound from his watch, followed by a startled shriek from Citizen Cruel.

"Oh no," they heard her yell. "Not more manure!"

Grandma Wrinkle and the Supreme Leader stared in disbelief at the holographic image, where they saw a dumpsterful of soggy leaves and brownish manure falling onto Citizen Cruel's head. They saw her hold her nose and leap to the top of the truck to avoid the rancid smell.

"Citizen Cruel, what is going on?" the Supreme Leader shouted.

"Oh, nothing, sir, that a little nose squeezing can't fix."

"I demand to know exactly what kind of vehicle you are riding in," the Supreme Leader asked.

"Well, sir, it's a very special kind of truck."

"Can it fly?"

"No, but there are thousands of flies in it."

"Stop talking in circles and tell me exactly what kind of special truck it is."

"Well, sir, on Earth they call it a garbage truck."

"As we do on our planet, you fool. Garbage is garbage no matter what galaxy you're in—except here we vacuum pack it and shoot it into space."

"Exactly, sir, which makes us infinitely more advanced than these earthlings."

"Some of us are, but clearly, not you."

"I am deeply sorry to have disappointed you, oh handsome and brilliant one," Citizen Cruel said. "Please, give me one more chance to return to the city of Hollywood and capture the boy."

"And how do you intend to do that in your garbage truck?"

"I'm thinking of creating a teleportation device using a four-legged, curly-haired creature they call a sheep."

"She's lying to you or she's just plain stupid," Grandma Wrinkle called out from her pod. "You can't ride sheep. They're too fluffy—the saddle will slide off."

"Who asked for your opinion, you old turtle?" the Supreme Leader snarled. He pulled his sword from its sheath on his belt. He waved it menacingly in the air. Grandma Wrinkle's eyes grew wide and her heart beat faster. She was old and ready to die, but not this way.

"How can you kill me, after all we've shared together?" she asked. "You're coldhearted to the core. You didn't used to be until you fell under the influence of that horrible Citizen Shady."

"He was my best friend when we were citizens-in-training."

"I was there too," Grandma Wrinkle said, "and I saw how much you wanted to be accepted by him. You gave up what you knew was right just to be in the power crowd. And now look at you."

"I learned everything I know from him."

"That's the problem. You learned everything you shouldn't know from him. You've forced your repressive laws on the entire planet. Go ahead and kill me with that sword of yours. At least I will have spoken my mind."

"I'm not going to kill you, at least not yet. I'm merely going to scratch my back with this sword. It gets to all the places my fingernails can't reach."

He rubbed the sword up and down his back, being careful to avoid his sensory enhancer, the trunk-like appendage on his back that all citizens of his planet had. Back in the day, it had made all the senses of his people operate at their best. But during his reign as Supreme Leader, he had ordered every citizen to have their sensory enhancers deactivated at the age of thirteen . . . except for his. He felt it was his right to keep all his senses and he didn't care what he denied his people. They lost all their sensory pleasures. To avoid that fate for her only grandson, Grandma Wrinkle, who was a master mechanic, had built a faster-than-light vehicle to send him to Earth on his thirteenth birthday. Now the Supreme Leader wanted him back to punish him and set a public example so no one would ever dare escape his planet again.

The Supreme Leader paced up and down, scratching his back as he always did when he was solving a problem.

"I can do this job," Citizen Cruel said. "Trust me. I will find the boy and bring him home."

The garbage truck lurched again. Grandma Wrinkle and the Supreme Leader saw Citizen Cruel fall down into the belly of the truck. As she reached out to regain her balance, she shrieked and backed up on all fours from some unknown threat.

"What's wrong with her?" Grandma Wrinkle said. "She looks like she saw a monster."

"I did," Citizen Cruel said. She pointed her holographic watch toward a mound of garbage nearby. A mother racoon and four little raccoons next to her were chewing on orange peels.

"That's what you're afraid of?" the Supreme Leader said. "A little furball? You are such a coward. No wonder you have failed in this mission."

The Supreme Leader threw his sword down so hard it stuck into the floor, barely missing Grandma Wrinkle's suction cup toes.

"That's it, you inadequate underling," he went on. "My patience has run out. I am coming to Earth to do what you clearly cannot do."

"But what about me?"

"I have a good mind to let your rot there in that garbage truck with the flies buzzing around your head."

"But, sir, you need me," Citizen Cruel was begging for her life. "It's dangerous here. Your body will never adapt to this environment. You will become weak, and your physical powers will not be what they are on our home planet."

"Need I remind you that my mind is strong?"

"Yes, but your body is old. And I mean that in the nicest possible way."

The Supreme Leader's six eyes flashed with anger. "Whatever I can do, it will be better than what you have managed to do in all the time that you've been there."

"You're forgetting one little thing, Clumsy," Grandma Wrinkle pointed out.

"Don't call me that in front of her," he said in a hoarse whisper.

"You'll need a spaceship," Grandma Wrinkle went on,

undaunted by his anger. "And I'm the only master mechanic on this planet who knows how to build one."

"How stupid do you think I am?" the Supreme Leader shouted. "Do you think I would have overlooked that? Right after your grandson escaped, I commissioned our leading scientist, Citizen Data-Head, to adapt one of our faster-than-light vehicles to make the long trip to Earth."

"That's not enough," Grandma Wrinkle smirked. "Earth's circumference is almost 25,000 miles around. What you don't know is where in all those miles my grandson is. Did you ever consider that?"

"Sir, you don't need to know his location," Citizen Cruel said. "I know it. I can take you to the boy."

"Fine," the Supreme Leader sighed. "Then I will be forced to keep you around a little bit longer. We will go together. Tell me, does the boy know what you look like?"

"Yes, he does."

"Then you'll need to disguise yourself so you don't give us away."

"I can do a biological alteration," Citizen Cruel said. She looked up at the sky through the open top of the truck and saw a regal red-tailed hawk circling above her. "I'll turn myself into a majestic hawk, and I will ride on your shoulder until it's time for me to pounce."

"There is nothing majestic about you," Grandma Wrinkle chimed in. "You're more like a pathetic, squawking parrot."

"Oh, shut up," Citizen Cruel said.

"Don't you tell her to shut up," the Supreme Leader said. "That's my job. And when I next see you, I will turn you into my pet parrot. Another brilliant idea of mine."

"It was my idea," Grandma Wrinkle protested. "But go ahead. Take credit for it, like you do for everything on this planet."

"You forget," Citizen Cruel said to the leader. "I am a shape-shifter. If you change me into a parrot, I will change myself back."

"No, you forget," he corrected her. "I am the Supreme Leader and my powers are greater than yours. You will remain a parrot as long as that is my wish. So it shall be."

That silenced Citizen Cruel. There was no way to respond to that.

"I will have Citizen Data-Head prepare to launch tonight," the Supreme Leader declared. "Get out of the garbage truck and send me the coordinates of where you are."

"I wouldn't trust anything she does," Grandma Wrinkle hissed. The Supreme Leader shot her a frown.

"As for you," he said, "I will deal with you and your rebellious grandson when I bring him home in chains."

"How are you going to punish her?" Citizen Cruel asked, laughing her cruel laugh that sounded like she had a chicken bone stuck in her throat. "I want to be there to see it."

"All the planet will see. It will be something they will never forget."

With a grand gesture, the Supreme Leader pulled his sword out of the ground and placed it back in its sheath. He snapped his fingers, and the prison wall opened for him to leave. Grandma Wrinkle was left alone in her pod to wonder what would become of her only and beloved grandson.

3

Buddy, they're waiting for you on set!" Rosa our wardrobe supervisor called, knocking on the door of my dressing room. "Get your costume on and hustle out there."

"Be there soon," I called back.

"Soon isn't soon enough. Duane is boiling over, and you know how cranky your director gets when you keep him waiting."

I didn't answer because I was concentrating hard on my biological alteration. As I said before, things weren't going well. I had managed to turn the left side of my body into my alien self, but my right side was still taking its own sweet time. To make matters worse, the sensory enhancer that grows from the middle of my back was acting up. It had gotten a whiff of my breakfast cinnamon bun, and it kept stretching its snout over to inhale the delicious aroma.

I don't usually speak to my body parts, but this was an emergency.

"You're not helping my transformation," I said to the enhancer. "You're going to get us in trouble if I don't get to rehearsal right away. Stop squirming and settle down."

I need mental focus to complete the biological alteration process that allows me to shift from human to alien and back again. With the amulet necklace clutched in the palm of my hand, I closed my three alien eyes on the left side and my one human eye on the right side and murmured the chant.

"*Be the real me. Be the real me*," I said over and over, sharpening my focus with each repetition. The transformation started to accelerate. I could feel my alien cobalt-blue skin creeping down my right side until it reached my human toes,

which transformed into my natural suction cups. My right hand grew seven spiny fingers with fingernails the length of lobster claws. (On my planet, we don't have lobsters, and I will never understand why you humans choose to eat them. They are so ugly. But then, I suppose you don't understand why we eat dung beetle antennae dipped in dried worm sweat, so I guess we're even.)

"Buddy!!" It was an angry voice from outside my door. "You're keeping the whole cast waiting. This is totally unacceptable!"

The door to my dressing room flew open, and our director, Duane Mitchell, marched in. He was so agitated that his ponytail was flapping from side to side. I hoped that he hadn't seen the last stages of my transformation. It's not pretty to see my human teeth disappear into my red alien gums.

"At least you're in your costume," Duane said. "Now let's go."

I breathed a sigh of relief as I let go of my amulet. If he had seen me half human, half alien, it would have been curtains for my show business career. He thinks I'm playing an alien, but he has no idea I actually am one. The only two humans who know that are my costar Cassidy Cambridge and my best friend, Luis Rivera.

"I'll just grab an avocado or two before we go on set," I said. "Avocados give me energy, you know."

"Oh, I didn't realize it was guacamole time," Duane snapped. "I'm so sorry I didn't bring you a bag of chips."

"Ah, that's okay, Duane. I can eat avocados solo."

"Don't get cute with me, son. Now let's move it. There's a show waiting to be made."

I followed Duane out of my dressing room and down the hall that led to the sound stage. We shoot our show, *Oddball Academy*, on Stage 42 at Universal Studios. We rehearse all week until Friday at four, when we do a dress rehearsal for a live audience. Then we have dinner together as a cast, get into makeup, and do the real show at seven. If this sounds like fun, it's because it is. More fun than you can even imagine. But it's also a lot of hard work, and Duane is the person who keeps us in line so we make the best show possible every week.

The cast and crew were all gathered on our set, hanging out in the school cafeteria, which is where a lot of the scenes take place. I sat down at one of the lunch tables where Cassidy was waiting. Just like Duane, she looked really annoyed. Even more annoyed was Tyler Stone, definitely the best-looking member of our cast. At least, according to him.

"Well, I guess we can begin now," Tyler said, "because his royal highness Buddy *Booger* has finally decided to show up."

"It's Burger," I said, "as in 'cheeseburger.'"

"Oh, so that's melted cheese dripping from your nose," Tyler snorted.

He laughed, and I was glad to see no one else in the cast did.

"Tyler, leave the comments to me," Duane snapped at him. "Last I checked, you weren't in charge. I'll be the only one talking on this set right now."

Tyler muttered something under his breath. I couldn't hear it, but I'm sure it was something nasty about me. Before I got my role on *Oddball Academy* over a month ago, he was the teen idol on the show. But then the fans started to notice me, and before I knew it, I had millions of followers on social media. I never tried to be more popular than him, it just happened, and now he was jealous of my popularity. Could I help it if I was the best-looking alien in this stratosphere?

No, I could not.

"Where were you?" Cassidy whispered to me. "Of all the days to be late, you had to pick the first day of rehearsal for our big special."

"I couldn't transform," I whispered back to her.

"Buddy, you know that this special could change the course of our whole careers. The network is giving us an entire hour on a whole other night, so more people will tune in to see us. That's how much confidence they have in us. I heard my mother talking to one of the network bosses on the phone. They said that if this special is a hit and gets a really big audience, they're going to give us our own movie to star in. Do you understand what that means?"

"Of course I understand what that means. Are you forgetting that I have all the books ever published stored in my brain and I can speak every language except Hungarian?"

"Yeah, but can you speak show business? It means we're going to be in theaters on a screen forty feet high instead of in people's living room on a screen that's fifty inches."

"Forty feet high! I better make sure I don't have guacamole stuck to my gums. It would look like gum fungus."

"Buddy, you say the weirdest things," Cassidy giggled.

I noticed that Duane was staring at us. I also noticed that he wasn't smiling.

"Whenever you two have finished laughing it up, I'd like to begin the rehearsal. Is that okay with you?"

"Oh yes," I answered enthusiastically. "I can't wait."

"He's being sarcastic, you doofus," Tyler snarled. "In case your thick brain didn't realize that."

"Hey, Tyler, lighten up," my fellow cast member Martha Cornfoot told him. She always defends me. "Buddy happens to be the smartest member of our cast."

"Yeah," my other cast pal Ulysses Park said. "He's like a regular Einstein."

Then he launched into a really bad German accent, which is his impression of the great scientist Albert Einstein. "Yah, zis is true. Buddy is zee second-schmartest person in zee vorld, after me. Gesundheit!"

"Wait," I said. "Isn't that what you say after someone sneezes? I didn't sneeze."

Ulysses shrugged. "It's the only German word I know. Besides, you will sneeze sometime in the future. Now you're covered."

"Okay, ladies and gentlemen," Duane said. "If we can cut the chatter and begin. I'd like you to open your scripts so we can get going. As you'll notice, the script is twice as long as usual. That's because we are doing an hour-long special."

"Oh man, sounds like we're going to be rehearsing all night," Tyler complained. "I can't stay late. I have an appointment to get a spray tan at five."

"Let me point out that the network is giving us a golden

opportunity to do a one-hour special and attract a huge audience," Duane explained. "And you, Mr. Stone, are worried about your tan. Do you see a problem with that?"

"I have a fan base that expects me to have a constant tan," Tyler said. "It's one of my best features."

"But Tyler," Cassidy said. "It's really hard to get the network to feature us. They're giving us a whole hour right after their highest-rated show so that all their viewers can discover us. And we get to do the show live. The only reason we got this special was because our ratings were so good from that episode a couple weeks ago, the one where we captured the pretend alien."

"*Entertainment Today* said it was the most exciting half hour of television in the last decade," Martha said. "They couldn't stop raving about how authentic it seemed. Almost like a real alien invasion."

Cassidy and I exchanged looks. We were the only cast members who knew that it actually was a real alien invasion. That horrible shape-shifter Citizen Cruel had been sent from my planet to kidnap me. Luckily, the cast and the audience sprang to my rescue and we all tied her up until the Center for Alien Studies could cart her away. I have no idea what they did with her, but wherever she is, they better watch her carefully, because she's a tricky, mean, unpredictable, vicious, merciless alien. But other than that, she's all heart.

"We were lucky that we have the greatest crew in the world who was able to capture it all on video," Duane said. "Our audience loved it, and I'm not going to let the network or our fans down. So let's get to work, people."

We opened our scripts and Duane asked Stan, the head writer, to introduce the script. Stan is a funny writer, but he talks better with his keyboard than in real life. He gets so nervous when he speaks that his mouth dries up and it sounds like he's got a wad of cotton balls tucked in there. I can relate. When I get nervous my mouth is so dry it feels like my two tongues get tied up in a knot.

I poured him a glass of water from my pitcher. I always keep a lot of water by me, because I have a huge need to constantly hydrate. I have to soak for several hours a day to keep my life force going on Earth. Maybe Stan had a little bit of alien in him too. He took about ten big gulps of water, then began.

"Th-th-this episode asks the question, Do Aliens Really Exist?" he stammered. "It was inspired by the person who invaded our set playing an alien. Although we all knew she was just an actress trying to get attention, it made us wonder:

what if she had been a real invading alien? What would we do? What would the students of *Oddball Academy* do?"

I noticed that Stan's mouth had moistened up quite a bit. When he talked about the show, he got so excited that he forgot about his nerves. His tongue was working just fine now. I was glad for him.

Ulysses stood up and did his best mechanical robot voice.

"I am an alien. Take me to your leader," he droned, then walked to Duane and said, "Hail, oh Supreme Leader."

That startled me. I spun all six eyes around and surveyed the whole stage. Had our Supreme Leader suddenly shown up? When I realized that Ulysses was just joking, my eyes stopped spinning and settled back down.

"Save that impression for the show," Duane said to Ulysses, while the rest of the cast laughed.

"Buddy, you play a friendly alien in the show," Stan said. "The question we ask in the show is are real aliens friendly or hostile? What would they do to our life here on Earth?"

I don't know why you humans are always so worried about hostile aliens. Most of us are really nice. The fish people of Aqua Ceti 13, for instance, gave our planet a huge supply of fried kelp when we had a food shortage. And the

Urlaks of Volpor are total sweethearts. The strongest citizens carry the weakest ones on their backs like two-legged taxis. And look at me. I couldn't be friendlier.

"On your feet, everyone," Duane said. "Let's block the opening scene. Buddy and Cassidy, you're at the lunch table. Ulysses and Martha, you're in the lunch line."

"And I assume I'm center stage, ready for my close-up," Tyler said.

"Actually, you're working behind the lunch counter," Duane said, "dishing up macaroni and cheese."

"Behind the counter?" Tyler groaned. "That doesn't work for me. My fans won't be able to see every inch of me. What do you think they tune in for? My pecs need to be front and center."

"We have a very important role for your pecs later in the show," Stan said. "Trust me, they have their own close-up."

That seemed to appease Tyler enough so that we could begin rehearsal. We took our places on the set and listened to Duane read the stage directions.

"We OPEN in the cafeteria," he read, "where the Oddball Academy students are gathered for lunch. Martha is singing the menu in an upbeat ode to fish sticks, while Buddy, our student alien, uses his fingernails to tap out the rhythm on the tabletop. Everyone looks up as we hear a whistle blow offscreen, and the new coach of the Oddball Academy athletic department enters stage left, wearing a track suit and carrying a clipboard."

We waited silently for what seemed to be a long minute.

"Where's the new guy?" Duane hollered. "Tell him he missed his cue."

We heard some rustling backstage, then the doors to the cafeteria burst open and the newest member of our cast, my pal Luis Rivera, entered. Luis was my first friend on Earth, and I managed to get him a minor role on our show. Luis spent the last year wearing a green rubber monster mask and taking pictures with the tourists as the lot's Frankenstein's monster. I was excited that I helped him get to do what he had always dreamed of doing: acting. He was the picture of enthusiasm. Unfortunately, he was a little too enthusiastic.

"Listen up, Oddballs," he shouted, leaping on top of one of the cafeteria tables and throwing both arms in the air.

"Today is our first belly ball practice. Remember, dudes and dudettes, you can only move the ball using your belly or your thigh." He grabbed the whistle from around his neck and gave it a long series of loud toots that nearly blew the headphones off Marcus, our sound guy.

"Cut rehearsal," Duane called out. "What do you think you're doing?" he asked Luis.

"Acting, sir!" Luis flashed a proud grin.

"Oh, is that what you call it?" Duane had an edge in his voice so sharp that it would cut you if you got too close. "Funny, I don't see anything in this script about your character shouting or jumping on a table or blowing a whistle so loud that it fries our eardrums."

"I'm just giving you the essence of my character," Luis said. "I researched his motivation, and I believe the whistle deeply defines who he is as a coach."

"Seriously?" Tyler said as he came out from behind the lunch counter. "We have to listen to this phony-baloney actor talk? Buddy, I can't believe you recommended this guy."

"Give him a break, Tyler," Cassidy said. "Luis will get better. This is his first day. He just needs to take it down a notch or two. "

"Or fifteen," Duane said.

"He'll be great," I said. "Cassidy and I can work with him."

"Fine," Tyler said. "While you guys do Acting for Kindergarteners here on set, I'm going to my dressing room. I have a very important meeting tomorrow and I have to prepare. In case you're interested—"

"Which we're not—" Ulysses interrupted, but Tyler went on anyway.

"I have received a handwritten invitation to meet with Howard Hitchcock, the fourth cousin twice removed of the world-famous classic film director, Alfred Hitchcock."

"Alfred Hitchcock? The guy they named Soundstage One after?" Martha said.

"None other. Apparently, his cousin is very interested in casting me as the lead in his next film."

"Oh, it must be a horror film," Ulysses said, and we all cracked up.

"I'm rubber, you're glue, whatever you say bounces off me and sticks to you," Tyler retorted.

"That's what my sister, Eloise, always says," Cassidy commented. "But she's seven."

Tyler turned to leave, shouting as he went. "Can someone bring me breakfast? Scrambled eggs, not too runny, toast, not too dark, and bacon, not too crisp."

Duane let out a loud sigh.

"Actually, Tyler, you don't have much to do in the opening

scene, so it wouldn't hurt for you to take a half-hour break. I don't want to interrupt your blossoming film career, but the set teacher needs you to bank some time in the classroom."

"Why? She's teaching us algebra this week, and who needs algebra when you have teeth like mine?"

He flashed his most teen-idol grin and headed in the direction of his dressing room before Janice, our set teacher, intercepted him and steered him to our classroom at the back of the soundstage.

"Come with me, young man," she said, taking him by the arm. "Algebra awaits."

"One day, you people will learn how to treat a star," I heard Tyler say as he was escorted away.

"And one day, you'll learn the importance of educating your brain," Janice said. She always gets the last word.

As the rest of us nonstars got to work, I held the script up to my head for seven seconds. I have the ability to read very quickly through my forehead.

"Wow," I said to Stan, bursting out into a gale of laughter. "This script is really great—so action-packed and funny."

"How do you know?" Stan asked. "We haven't even read through it yet."

The other cast members stared at me, waiting for an answer. Since most of them didn't know my real identity, telling them that I could speed-read through my forehead was not an option. Or was it? Sometimes the truth is so strange it's hard to believe. I gave it a whirl.

"Well you know, we aliens can read a whole book just by holding it up to our foreheads," I said. "You should try it sometime."

Everyone laughed and held their scripts up to their heads.

"Not working for me," Martha said.

"Try this," Ulysses said, putting the script on his chair and sitting on it. "This works. I can read with my butt. It's already on page 33."

Everyone was cracking up but Duane.

"This is all fun and games," he said, "but it's not getting our special on the air. So how about we get our foreheads and our butts out of the way and read the script the old-fashioned way with just our plain old eyes. Eyes on the script, bodies on the set."

I moved all six of my plain old eyes to page one and we began our work in earnest.

4

ODDBALL ACADEMY
Hour Special
"The Day the Aliens Came to Visit"
Written by Stan Edwards

INT. CAFETERIA — DAY

We OPEN in the cafeteria where the Oddball Academy students are gathered for
lunch. Martha is singing the menu in an
upbeat ode to fish sticks, while Buddy,
our student alien, uses his fingernails
to tap out the rhythm on the tabletop.

                    MARTHA (singing)
        Fish sticks are smelly
        And hurt my belly
        Tell me why
        They're always for lunch
        Where is the pizza
        We want to munch?

Her song is interrupted as we hear a
WHISTLE blowing offscreen. The new coach
of the Oddball Academy athletic department enters stage left, wearing a track-
suit and carrying a clipboard.

                    COACH
        Hey, kids. Let's get out on the
        field. Today is our first belly
        ball practice.

                    CASSIDY
        What's belly ball? It sounds dumb.

                    MARTHA
        And flabby.

COACH

It's a game I invented. Perfect for
you oddballs. You can only move
the ball using your belly or your
thigh.

CASSIDY

Why can't we just play volleyball
like other regular kids?

ULYSSES

Because we're not regular. We're
oddballs. Cassidy, you see the future, Buddy's an alien from the
second ring of Saturn, Martha's
convinced she's a Broadway musical
star, and I channel famous people
from history. By the way, here's a
touch of my Abraham Lincoln impression . . .
        (in a high, nasal voice)
"Four score and seven years ago,
our fathers brought forth . . ."

MARTHA

Wait a minute. You sound like
you're talking through a snorkel.
I didn't know Abraham Lincoln gave
his speeches underwater.

ULYSSES

Stick with me and I'll make history
come alive.

CASSIDY

Whether or not it happened.

COACH

Right now, my little oddkins, we've
got a ball game to prepare for.
    (pointing to Buddy)
You with the seven fingers, I'm
going to make you the goalie. You
got the hands for it. Just be careful not to puncture the ball with
those nails.

                    BUDDY
No worries, Coach. I'm a trained
athlete. On my planet, I'm a ping-
pong champion. I use my nails for
paddles.

                    COACH
Okay, chow down on those fish
sticks, and I'll meet you on the
field in fifteen minutes.

                   ULYSSES
But, Coach, that doesn't even give
us time to digest.

                    COACH
That's the point. You can use your
stomach gas as a weapon.

AS the students look at the fish sticks
and groan, we CUT TO:

EXT. ATHLETIC FIELD — DAY

The Oddball Academy kids are on the
field, trying to pass the ball from belly
to belly. The coach is blowing his whistle, yelling commands.

                    COACH
          Cassidy, stick your belly out.
          You gotta have an aggressive
          belly pass. And Buddy, guard the
          goal with your thigh.

                    BUDDY
          But Coach, it hurts. I'm turning
          black and blue.

                    COACH
          What's the problem? You're already
          blue.

Suddenly, there is RUMBLING offscreen,
and all the students look up into the

sky. A doughnut hole starts to form and the sky opens like a portal.

> CASSIDY
> (still looking up to the sky)
> What is that?

> ULYSSES
> (in a Superman voice)
> It's a bird. It's a plane. It's SUPERMAN!

Suddenly, a face forms in the doughnut hole, peering down at them. It is the face of the alien who invaded the set of *Oddball Academy*.

> MARTHA
> Correction. It's Superwoman. And she's looking angry.

> COACH
> How do you know?

MARTHA

She's sticking her two tongues out
at us. Buddy, is she from your
planet?

BUDDY

The citizens of my planet are
peaceful. They would never stick
their tongues out at strangers.

ULYSSES

Everyone knows aliens are weird and
want to capture humans to do exper-
iments on us.
    (does an impression in an alien
    voice)
"Come with me, my little lab rat.
We will see what makes you tick."

CASSIDY

Why don't we try to talk to the
alien first? Maybe we're judging
her too quickly. What if she's

really nice and can teach us some
outer-space dances?

MARTHA

Yeah, and I can teach her some
songs. Like "Space Oddity," I bet
she'd relate to that. Or "Rocket
Man."

Martha bursts into song, a very bluesy
rendition.

MARTHA (con't)

"It's so lonely out in space . . ."

ULYSSES

Whoa, put a cork in it, Martha! If
she hears you singing, she'll leave
and we'll never get a chance to
meet a real alien.

COACH

Don't get too cocky, kids. We don't

know if she's friendly. Buddy, you
got any intel for us?

BUDDY

I've never seen her before, but she
looks like one of the Ecuts of
Zoron.

ULYSSES

Uh oh. Look, that Ecut, or whatever
she is, is coming toward us, and
she's scratching her armpit.

CASSIDY

Eeuuww. I hope she doesn't touch me
with that hand. I don't want her
alien sweat touching my skin.

BUDDY

The armpit thing isn't a good sign.
The Ecuts don't eat their prey with
their mouths. They absorb them
through their armpits.

                    COACH

That means she thinks we're prey.

                    MARTHA

And we're going to get sucked into
her armpits and have to smell them
forever and ever.

                    COACH

No way! Let's get outta here, kids.
Run!

                    ULYSSES

Where to?

                    COACH

Anyplace an armpit can't get you!

The entire belly ball team scatters like
mice, heading offstage in every direction, screaming for help.
          CUT TO:

5

Cassidy and I were in the middle of a hot debate when we walked into the house after rehearsal that day. Cassidy's mom, Delores, who became my manager when I got the job on *Oddball Academy*, had picked us up at the studio, as usual. I live with Cassidy's mom and little sister in their house in the Hollywood Hills because everyone thinks my parents are on an archeological dig in the desert. It was, of course, a totally made-up story. I had seen this archeologist called Indiana Jones in a bunch of movies I watched in secret with my Grandma Wrinkle back on my home planet, so I guess I had archeology on the brain.

As we walked into the house, I was in a hurry to get into my bathtub and submerge. If I don't soak in water for at least an hour a day, my life force starts to drain out of me. I could already feel my energy fading from the long day of rehearsals, but Cassidy needed to talk, and I had things to say too.

"I just don't know why they always have to show aliens as bad guys," I said as we walked into the kitchen. "Stan is really funny, but his views on aliens are so narrow. It offends me personally. I need to talk to him about a rewrite."

"But Buddy," Cassidy made her way to the refrigerator and got a chocolate ice-cream bar from the freezer. "I think the script is so exciting. It's got everything: an alien with two tongues, an eating armpit, and a run for our lives."

Cassidy took the wrapper off the ice-cream bar and put it around the stick to catch any drops of dribbling chocolate.

"I tell you, Buddy. We're going to crush the ratings, and by this time next year, we're going to be movie stars."

"Not if you keep eating like that," Delores said, snatching the ice-cream bar out of Cassidy's hands. "Remember, the camera makes every actor seem ten pounds heavier."

"Mom, I was eating that," Cassidy protested.

"And you will, just a little less of it."

Delores took a kitchen knife out of the drawer, sliced off the top half of the ice-cream bar, and tossed it down the garbage disposal.

"Mom!" cried Eloise, Cassidy's seven-year-old sister,

who was building a Lego castle at the kitchen table with her dad. "You can't throw that away. I'm standing right here. That was chocolate-chocolate chip, my favorite."

"Everybody knows that salted caramel ribbon is the best flavor," Cassidy's dad said.

"That is your father's opinion," Delores said to the girls, "which I do not share."

"We know, Mom," Cassidy groaned. "You guys never have the same opinion about anything."

"Except loving you girls," Mr. Cambridge said.

"Is salted caramel ribbon the reason you're getting divorced?" Eloise asked. "Because I can make room for both flavors in the freezer."

"That sounds like a great idea," I said. "I'll help you rearrange the freezer right after my bath. Then you can move back in, Mr. Cambridge."

"Thanks, Buddy, but it's not quite that simple. There are a lot of other adult things we have to work out."

"Oh," I said knowingly. "Like who controls the TV remote."

"Something like that." He smiled.

"And who gets to take Eloise to Space Camp this week," Delores said.

"I already told you guys," Eloise said, "I'm not going to Space Camp. I don't like sleeping away. It gives me the creeps."

"But your whole class is going, pumpkin," Mr. Cambridge said. "And your teacher assured us that your best friend, Maisy, will be in your bunk. Won't that be fun?"

"For her, maybe, but not for me. I'll just stay up all night thinking about creepy things like outer-space aliens."

"Aliens can be really nice," I said to Eloise. "Look at me."

"You're just a pretend alien, Buddy. And by the way, why don't you go take your costume off. That thing on your back is so gross."

That insult must have hurt my sensory enhancer's feelings, because it peeked out from under my arm and made a grunting sound

"Why do you make it do that?" Eloise said, jumping on her father's lap. "It sounds like your arm is farting. Take the batteries out."

"Buddy's costume is a pretty fancy piece of technology," Mr. Cambridge said. "It's nothing to be scared of. It's something to appreciate."

"It looks itchy and I don't like it. And I don't like Space Camp either. Not even a little bit."

"What if Mom or Dad goes with you?" Cassidy said,

licking the last little bit of chocolate off the stick. "When I was your age, I didn't want to go Dance Camp and Mom came with me for the first night. After that, I loved it."

"Don't even bring that up," Delores said instantly, "because I can't go with her this week. It's out of the question. You're taping the big special and my services are needed on the set."

"No, they're not, Delores," I said. "The main thing you do on set is stand around and watch your daughter. I can do that really well. I've got six eyes."

Delores slammed her coffee cup down on the counter so hard that half the coffee flew out. "That's gratitude for you," she said. "I am highly involved in protecting both of your careers. Who do you think got you those lovely throw pillows for the couch in your dressing room?"

"The ones that make me sneeze?"

"Yes, but they add a pop of color to an otherwise drab environment."

"Well, if you can't go, maybe Daddy can go with me to Space Camp," Eloise said. "Daddy, please, please, please."

Mr. Cambridge took Eloise in his arms and gave her a big hug. I thought he was going to say yes, but he surprised us all.

"I would love to go with you, pumpkin, but I have to

present my blueprints for the museum addition to the board of directors this week. I've been working on the architectural plans for months, and I can't miss the presentation."

"Who cares about a stupid old museum?" Eloise said, getting off his lap.

"I do. I'm an architect and I care about making a beautiful building for our city."

"It's not fair, Daddy. I hate museums and I hate art. And I hate Space Camp."

I felt bad for little Eloise. I know what it's like to be away from home and miss everyone you care about, even if it's for just one night.

"I can teach you all about space right here," I said to her. "I know way more than you think I know. Like, did you know that the brightest star in the night sky is called Sirius and it's one of the closest stars to Earth at a distance of 8.6 light-years away."

"I don't care, I hate space too!" Eloise burst into tears. "The only reason to go to Space Camp is for the s'mores."

S'mores? That was a new word for me, and I ran it through my mental Earth dictionary, which only takes a nanosecond. I learned that the word "s'more" is a contraction of the phrase "some more." It's a crazy-delicious food, and the recipe was first developed in the early twentieth century. It's a sandwich of two graham crackers, toasted marshmallow, and half a melted chocolate bar.

My eyes zoomed around my head at just the thought of such a food. You humans will stop at nothing to satisfy your sweet tooth. On my planet, we only have tasteless nutritional wafers to eat. I made a mental note to make up a batch of s'mores one day and eat fifty or a hundred of them.

"How about if we make s'mores right here in the living room," I said. "We have fireplace."

"That's a hard no," Delores said. "No s'mores. No fireplace. No Space Camp at home. Eloise is going to Space Camp, and that's final."

"But I can't go alone," Eloise said. She dropped to the floor, pounding her little fists on the tile and wailing like an injured hyena.

"Is she okay?" I whispered to Cassidy.

"She's fine. It's just a tantrum."

"I am not fine," Eloise shrieked, grabbing me by my legs. "Don't let them take me. Don't make me go alone."

I had never seen a human tantrum before, and it was fascinating. On my planet, the children are all well-behaved, and when we turn thirteen and our sensory enhancer is deactivated, we don't feel anything. All the citizens walk around like zombies. I tried to put myself in Eloise's skin to feel what a tantrum feels like. I threw myself down on the floor and started wailing with her.

"Don't make us go alone!" I cried. "Please, take pity on us."

Delores, Mr. Cambridge, and Cassidy all stared at me like I had lost my mind. Even Eloise couldn't believe what she was seeing. She stopped her tantrum midwail.

"Wait a minute, Buddy, this is MY tantrum. You can have your own later."

"Okay," I said. "That's fair."

I got up from the floor, and Eloise picked up where she left off, kicking her feet and howling loudly.

"Mom, can you please help out a little here," Cassidy said. "My eardrums are about to explode."

"All right," Delores sighed. "You win, Eloise. I will ask your teacher if I can come to Space Camp with you, but for one night only."

"Really, Mommy?" Eloise stopped howling as quickly as she had started, and a smile spread across her cute little face. "Can we share a seat on the bus?"

"Now you're pushing it, little lady. I'm not the bus type, particularly when there are carsick children barfing up their lukewarm tuna sandwiches around me. And second of all, I warned you that I'm only staying one night."

"But I'm afraid of buses too."

"Fine. I'll go on the bus, and I'll have a car pick me up the next day. If I go on Wednesday for the first night, then I'll be back home on Thursday and still be here for the dress rehearsal and the taping on Friday."

"You're the best mommy in the world!" Eloise threw her arms around Delores. "I'm going to go pack and make sure I can fit Miss McCuddles into my backpack."

"It's going to be hard to fit a whole human into that little backpack," I pointed out.

"Buddy, you're so funny," she laughed. I'm not sure why because I wasn't making a joke. "Miss McCuddles is my stuffed unicorn. She goes everywhere with me."

I watched Eloise skip happily down the hall to her

bedroom. I presumed that meant the tantrum was over, until I heard a bloodcurdling scream come from her bedroom.

"I can't find Miss McCuddles!" she shrieked. "She's lost and I'm going to miss her forever and ever."

"This is one I can fix," Mr. Cambridge said. "I saw Miss McCuddles hanging out with the dust bunnies under the bed." He headed down the hall but stopped and turned back to us. "Thanks, Delores. I'll make it up to you sometime."

"That sometime will be Friday," Delores said. "I need to be on set every second. Cassidy's entire movie career is riding on this special. Nothing can go wrong."

I felt a wave of dizziness sweep over me. Maybe it was the sudden anxiety of realizing that we had to make a perfect show.

"Buddy, you don't look so good," Cassidy whispered to me. "Should I get you an avocado?"

"We're all out," Delores said. "I ate the last one for lunch with a little shrimp and Russian dressing. It was delicious."

That wasn't good news. In order to survive on Earth, I need a daily long soak in water and a lot of avocados. Cassidy and I discovered that they have all the nutrients I need to survive.

"Mom, could I ask you to go to the market and get

some more avocados," Cassidy said. "You know how Buddy loves them."

"I'll get them tomorrow."

"No, now!" I heard myself say with desperation in my voice. I had waited too long and my energy was sinking to nothing. I felt like I was going to pass out.

"Well, look who's being rude," Delores snapped. "You sound like Tyler. Bring me this, get me that. Trust me, Buddy, that kind of star behavior will get you nowhere fast. The universe doesn't center around you."

"Delores, not to be rude, but there is no center of the universe. It started with the big bang fourteen thousand million years ago and has been expanding ever since."

"Thank you, Mr. Space Camp. It was just a figure of speech."

"I have an idea, Mom," Cassidy said. "How about if you take a quick trip to the market, and Buddy and I can use the time to run our lines for tomorrow's rehearsal. Dad's here to watch Eloise, and we need to seriously rehearse. We want to be fantastic for the special, don't we, Buddy?"

The room was starting to spin and Cassidy's voice sounded far away.

"Just nod your head," she whispered to me.

"What?"

"Nod your head, up and down. Like this."

I did.

"I like the sound of that," Delores said. "I'm glad you kids are finally starting to realize how hard actors have to work to make it look easy." She picked up her car keys. "I'll be back soon. Work hard."

"Can you also pick up some carrot sticks for me," Cassidy asked.

"I like the sound of that too," Delores said.

As soon as Delores was out the door, Cassidy grabbed me by the arm. It was just in time, because another two minutes and I would have flopped over on my face.

"Go on," she said. "Get in the bath. Soak as long as you need to. I'll cover for you until the avocados arrive."

I was barely able to stagger to my bathroom and turn on the tub's taps. As I crawled into the warm water, I let out a deep sigh.

Life on Earth was both wonderful and terrible, and at that moment, I wasn't sure which was which.

6

"**O**kay, everyone," Duane called out, looking at his watch. "It's eleven o'clock and you've done really good work, so let's take a hard fifteen-minute break. I hear Mary has whipped up something special for us."

"That's right. I've got my homemade pizza bites . . . with sausage for you meat lovers and mushrooms for the veggie eaters."

It was Tuesday, and we were on the set, where we had been rehearsing since nine o'clock that morning. We had blocked most of the show the day before, but we still had three scenes to go, including the final scene when the aliens take off to return to their planet. It takes a lot of concentration because you're holding your script, reading your lines, taking notes in the margin, and learning your moves all at the same time. Fortunately, Luis had brought me a snack of guacamole from his grandmother's restaurant.

I was going to need every last morsel of that avocado dip to keep my mind and body sharp for the rest of the day.

While Mary was passing around a tray of her pizza snacks, Luis handed me the plastic container of guacamole with a bag of homemade chips. When I'm not in my human form, I have no teeth, only bright red gums. That makes the eating of chips a little painful. If you've ever been poked in the gums by a corn chip, you know what I'm talking about.

"I presoaked the chips for you in some warm water, dude," Luis whispered, pulling up a director's chair and flopping himself down next to me. "We got to protect those alien gums of yours."

Other than Cassidy, Luis is the only person who knows my true alien identity, and they've both been great about keeping it secret. We all agreed that no one else can know, or the government could lock me up and take me to a secret alien study center I hear they have. Sometimes I wonder if that's where they took Citizen Cruel. She hasn't been heard from since she was captured and carried off our set.

I took one of the soggy chips and tried to load it with guacamole, but it collapsed under the weight. The mess I was creating didn't go unnoticed by Tyler, who was busy scarfing down most of the pizza bites before anyone else could get to them.

"That's disgusting," Tyler commented through a mouthful of cheesy mushrooms. "Try keeping your mouth closed when you chew."

"You should take your own advice," Luis replied. "You got some nasty fungus hanging from your mouth."

"That's called a mushroom, doofus."

"For your information, a mushroom is a fungus." Luis looked very proud of himself for having that information.

"It takes one to know one," Tyler said. Then he burst out laughing, thinking he had just said something really clever. He reached out to the tray and scooped up another handful of pizza bites.

"Whoa, Tyler, slow down. Those are for everybody," Mary snapped. "Didn't your parents teach you any manners?"

"My parents taught me that I'm the star here, which means I can have as many pizza bites as I want."

"Not from this tray," Mary said, picking it up from the table and carrying it over to the camera crew.

Duane asked if he could see Luis for a few minutes in his office. He wanted to work with him on his performance, which was still pretty over the top. The rest of us sat down in a circle, munching on our snacks together. They say when you work on a show with the same people every day, you develop a rhythm that makes you almost move as one unit. There we were, all chewing as if we were one person.

"Okay, gang," Ulysses said. "One the count of three, we swallow together. One . . . Two . . . *Gulp*."

And we did. Just as we were loading up our mouths for Round Two, our stage guard, Hudson Goodman, came up to us.

"Excuse me for interrupting your snack," he said.

"Help yourself, Hudson," Mary called out. "You know you can't resist my piping-hot pizza bites."

"Save me some for later," he said. "Right now, I'm here to say that you have a very distinguished guest waiting outside. He said he's the world renown director Howard Hitchcock and he has a meeting with Tyler Stone."

Tyler popped out of his chair and wiped the mushroom juice off his face with page eleven of his script.

"Hey," Stan said to him. "You just wiped your mouth with my best joke."

"No disrespect, man," Tyler said. "But the guy I'm about to meet makes this script seem like baby talk. He is a master of suspenseful dialogue. If you hang with me, maybe I can get you an introduction."

"How about me?" Martha said. "Wouldn't Mr. Hitch-cock like to meet a master of musical comedy?"

"He directs murder mysteries, Martha, not comedies."

"No problem. My high notes are killers."

"Tyler, would you like me to bring him in?" Hudson asked. "Or are you coming out to meet him?"

"You can bring him here," Tyler said. "I'll be generous and let all you guys have a look at him before we go to my dressing room. It might be the closest you'll ever come to meeting a real film director. You can thank me later."

"By the way," Hudson said. "Just so you won't be shocked. He's not alone."

"Oh, did he bring his head of casting?" Tyler asked. He winked at all of us. "That'll save me a meeting."

"Uh . . . not exactly," Hudson stammered. "Unless the head of casting has wings and a beak."

Hudson hurried out and returned two minutes later, followed by one of the strangest sights I'd ever seen. I mean, Hollywood is known for strange people, but Mr. Howard Hitchcock took the prize.

7

Howard Hitchcock looked like no other human I'd ever seen. He was wearing a long trench coat buttoned to the neck and leather riding boots covering his very small feet. His hands were stuffed into fur-lined leather gloves with a silver snap at the wrist. On his head, he wore what I think is called a pith helmet, the kind of hard hat people wear on a safari, and hanging from it was a blue mosquito net that covered his face. He had very bad posture, because he had what seemed like a hump in the middle of his back. Obviously, his mother had never told him to stand up straight. Grandma Wrinkle always said to me, "Shoulders back, chins up."

But the strangest thing of all about him was that a bright-green parrot was riding on his shoulder. It was no small parrot, either, but a big, hefty bird with a sharp beak and flashing golden eyes. And, I should add, a very

bad personality. I usually get
along with animals, but this
feathered creature took one
look and me and squawked,
"Hello, loser."

Everyone's head snapped
around in my direction.

"Why would you say that
to me?" I asked the bird. "You
don't even know me."

"I know you! I know you!"
The bird's voice sounded shrill
and unpleasant.

"No you don't, no you
don't!" I snapped back in the
same parrot-like voice.

"Hey, Buddy," Ulysses said. "Impressions are my terri-
tory. Stay out unless you're invited."

"Besides, you're arguing with a bird," Cassidy pointed
out. "It doesn't even know what it's saying."

"*Squawk!* Shut up, girlie! *Squawk!*"

The director glared at the parrot on his shoulder and
poked it so hard in the chest that the bird nearly fell off
his shoulder.

"Close your beak, Zelda," he commanded. "Now, which one of you is Tyler Stone, the heartthrob I've heard so much about?"

"Obviously, I am," Tyler said. "I'm the best-looking one here."

"Ah," said Mr. Hitchcock. "And what exactly makes you so?"

"If you took that net off, it would all become clear."

"I have very sensitive eyes and they need to be shielded at all times," the director said. His voice sounded vaguely familiar. I thought maybe I had seen him once in a movie back home.

"Well then, let me help your eyes out," Tyler said. "Notice my abs and my pecs, which resemble that Roman god, what's his name, you know, the one who carries that awesome hammer thing."

"That would be Thor," Ulysses said. "Who wasn't a Roman but a Norse god."

"Norse?" Tyler said. "Where is Norse? Never heard of the place. It sounds like a direction."

Although I hated to be in the same category as Tyler, intelligence-wise, I had never heard the word "Norse" before either. I ran it through my Earth dictionary, which told me that it refers to the people and language of Norway who lived between the seventh and fifteenth centuries. I happily shared this fact with the assembled group. Mr. Hitchcock turned his face to me and gave me a dark look.

"Who are you?" he asked. "And where do you come from, to have such deep knowledge of human history?"

"Arizona!" I blurted out. It was the first thing I thought of because the night before I had just seen a commercial for a planned senior citizen community called Sunny Living that was in Arizona.

"Buddy," Martha said. "I thought you said you were from Wisconsin."

"I am," I said. "Wisconsin, Arizona. It's a very small town you've probably never heard of. It's famous for its big cheese statue of a horse."

"*Squawk!*" the parrot screeched. "Don't believe him! *Squawk!*"

"Excuse me, Mr. Hitchcock, but you need to teach your parrot some manners," Martha said. "He is extremely rude."

"The parrot is a she."

"Whatever. She's got a mean mouth."

"Yes she does," the director answered. Then, turning to the bird and giving her another hard poke, which almost knocked her off his shoulder a second time, he said, "If you can't behave, I'll have to cage you again."

"Oh please don't do that," Cassidy said. "I hate to see animals in cages. They're living creatures who should be able to express themselves in freedom, with joy."

When she said that, I think Cassidy might have even had a little tear in her eye. She has such a warm heart. Mr. Hitchcock noticed too.

"And who are you, my lovely delicate flower?" he asked.

"That's Cassidy Cambridge, sir," I piped up. "America's teenage sweetheart and the star of our show. Also one of my best friends."

"I'm pleased to meet you, Cassidy," Mr. Hitchcock said. "We'll have to talk more about your career."

He reached out and shook her hand, holding it for a long moment. Cassidy must have been overwhelmed at meeting such an important director, because I think I saw a little shudder go down her arm. She just stood there smiling a kind of goofy smile.

"Your handshake feels positively electric," she said.

"You're not the first person to notice that," he said. "It's an extension of my powerful personality."

"I see what you mean," Cassidy said. He held on to her hand for another ten seconds until he finally let it go. Tyler noticed their obvious connection and immediately wedged himself between Cassidy and Mr. Hitchcock.

"If you remember correctly, I think it was me you came to see," he said to the director. "Let's talk in private in my dressing room. I'll order us a bowl of Cheez-Its and pretzels."

"Are those foods?" Mr. Hitchcock asked.

"Some people call them that," Cassidy said. "My mom, Delores, calls them empty calories."

"Did somebody say my name?" That would be Delores, who had emerged from Cassidy's dressing room, her gold bracelets clanking against one another like a symphony of jewelry. Undoubtedly, she had come to request more lines for Cassidy. She spends a lot of our rehearsal time counting each of our lines and making sure Cassidy has at least one more than everyone else.

Delores stopped suddenly when she saw Mr. Hitchcock. She looked him up and down and made no attempt to hide her shock at his appearance.

"I was just talking with your lovely daughter about her career," Mr. Hitchcock said.

"Oh, were you? Well, if you want to talk to my daughter, you talk to me first. I'm her manager and her career goes through me. Frankly, given the way you're dressed, I don't think we want to work with you."

"Delores," I said. "This is Mr. Howard Hitchcock, the fourth cousin twice removed of the renowned director Alfred Hitchcock. He's also an important film director."

Delores' attitude changed instantly. She turned on the charm faster than you could say *That's Hollywood for you!*

"How nice that you want to chat with my daughter," she said, her red, glossy lips breaking into a big smile. "Cassidy and I have always admired your work in the film industry, Henry."

"It's Howard."

"Of course it is, Howard. And my, what a lovely bird you have. He is such a unique accessory."

"She," Mr. Hitchcock corrected.

"Oh really? How interesting. So about Cassidy's career— you were saying?"

"Excuse me, Delores, but Mr. Hitchcock is here to see me," Tyler said, taking the director by the arm. "He thinks I'm the one with big-screen potential."

"He'll learn," Delores said. "You boys go right ahead and have your little conversation. When Mr. Hitchcock gets bored with you, I think he'll come to realize my clients are the ones with the real talent around here."

"Clients?" asked Mr. Hitchcock.

"Yes, Cassidy and Buddy Burger here. He is fabulous at playing aliens. So natural."

Mr. Hitchcock turned his attention to me.

"Yes, he does look like a real alien."

"How would you know?" Delores asked.

"You don't want to know how I know," he said, mimicking her. "So, Buddy, have you been working on this show for very long?"

"Only about six weeks, sir," I said.

"Ever since you came from . . . where was it again?"

Oh no. What had I said? Was it Arizona or Wisconsin?

"Arizona." Cassidy jumped in, saving me as usual.

"Well, Buddy, I'm sure we'll meet again," Mr. Hitchcock said. "One way or another. Shall we go, Tyler?"

"Cheez-Its coming right up," he said, as they hurried toward his dressing room. I could hear Zelda squawking, "Zelda wants a Cheez-It! Zelda wants a Cheez-It!" as they headed down the hall.

Duane returned with Luis to get our rehearsal going again. But even as we worked on the next scene, Mr. Hitchcock's words kept rolling around in my head.

"'We'll meet again, one way or the other,'" I repeated to Cassidy on our next break. "I wonder what he meant by that. It sounded more like a threat than an invitation."

"Oh, Buddy," Cassidy said. "You've seen too many scary movies. You get the creeps from everything."

She was right. I do worry about too many things. And I have seen too many scary movies. And my creepy meter is always running on high. But there was something about Mr. Hitchcock—maybe it was the tone of his voice or the way he shook hands or his mysterious way of dressing—that told me this time, my creepy meter just might be right.

8

When Tyler was finished with his meeting with Howard Hitchcock, he came bursting back onto the set, interrupting our rehearsal without even so much as an "excuse me."

"Guys," he said. "That meeting was better than I ever expected. You're looking at the star of Howard Hitchcock's next box office smash, *The Prince and the Beast.*"

"I assume you're playing the beast," Ulysses said.

"Ulysses, little dude, your attempt at humor is not appreciated," Tyler said. "I'll remember that when I'm a movie star casting my own productions."

Duane looked terribly annoyed. Actually, furious would be a better word.

"You might not have noticed, Tyler, but we are in the middle of rehearsing a scene here. And you're in it."

"How can you compare what just happened to me with this little show?" Tyler said. He picked up his script, which was waiting for him on the table. "I mean, this is only 54 pages. A movie script is 110 pages. And most of them will feature me, as the strikingly handsome prince who must overcome the jealous beast and win the hand of the fair maiden. By the way, Cassidy, he wants to talk to you as a possibility to play the maiden."

"Me?" Cassidy said. "Did he specifically say my name?"

"He asked my opinion about your acting chops, and I told him that with training, you had possibilities. Obviously, I have the charisma but with me as your acting partner, you could shine."

"Cass, that's great," I said. "I'm sure Mr. Hitchcock sees a big future for you."

"For us," Tyler said. Turning to Cassidy, he added. "There's no you without me."

The conversation was interrupted by Duane slamming his script down on the table and clapping his hands together loudly to get our attention.

"Excuse me, people," he shouted. "I need you here now, paying attention to *this* script and *this* show, which just happens to be shooting *this* Friday. After that, you'll have a lifetime to discuss your future careers . . . or lack of same."

Duane's anger made me very uncomfortable. On my planet, we are not allowed to show sudden bursts of anger, or in fact, sudden bursts of anything, including joy, excitement, or happiness. Only the Supreme Leader and his Squadron are allowed to blow up, which they do quite often. The rest of us are expected to keep our emotions in check at all times. I am amazed that here in Hollywood people can say what they feel and not get put in a prison pod or be shot into space forever.

"Tyler, I know you feel this little 54-page script is beneath you," Duane went on, "but let's see if you can try to concentrate on it. We are rehearsing scene four. You and Luis are on the playing field when you see the alien ship land."

"Who's Luis?"

"Luis, the actor who's playing the coach."

"Oh, that guy? You want me to act with him? Are you forgetting I'm a movie star?"

"Tyler," Duane sighed. "You've been a movie star for exactly three minutes. Besides, Luis is coming along nicely. Buddy's going to run lines with him this afternoon so he can improve even more. Now with your permission, let's get back to this little thing we call work. Places, everyone!"

We took our places on the set. It wasn't our usual classroom or cafeteria set, which are permanent. This was a swing set, a specially built location just for the episode we were shooting that week. This one looked like a soccer field, with fake grass, a bench on each side for the players, fake trees that the prop people rolled in, and pools of blinking lights shining down that were supposed to be from the spaceship.

"Let's start from page 15," Duane said. "Luis, give yourself a count of three and then enter."

Offstage, I could hear Luis counting to three. I don't think anyone else could hear him, but my sensory enhancer, which amplifies all of my senses, allowed my ears to pick up his whispered voice. I felt nervous watching him make his entrance because I was the one who talked Duane into hiring him. But as it turned out, I didn't need to be nervous. Luis was vastly improved from the day before. It was like he was tiny little Mercury yesterday, and today he was giant gassy Jupiter. Working with Duane had really helped him.

"Gather round, team," he said as he took his place in the middle of the fake grass. "This is the last belly ball practice before the big game. I want us to work as a unit and pull together. Keep victory foremost in your mind."

"Excuse me, Coach," Ulysses read from his script.

"But there seems to be a large flying saucer blinking its lights at us."

Luis looked up intothe lighting grid above us and did a double take that was very funny and dramatic at the same time. He really looked like he had seen a flying saucer. By the way, I need to point out that real spaceships do not look anything like flying saucers. I don't know where you humans got that idea. I mean, a saucer is handy if you want to put your cup of hot tea down, but they certainly do not catapult through space. My Grandma Wrinkle built lots of faster-than-light crafts, and not one of them looked like something you'd have a tea and cookie with.

"Show of hands, everyone," Luis said. "How many here vote to run as fast as we can and hide? Hmmm . . . Forget the vote. Run for your lives!"

"Hold it right there!" Duane hollered and we turned away from our scripts to face him. "Luis, that's much improved. Your work is paying off."

I felt such a surge of pride in Luis. I knew he had the talent in him. I flashed him one of my red-gum smiles and winked at him with three of my six eyes. He gave me a very cool thumbs-up.

Duane began to block the next part of the scene, explaining to us how we were supposed to react to the spaceship by running off the set, each character heading toward one of the cameras. As he was showing us our moves, Hudson the guard came in and cleared his throat loudly to get Duane's attention.

"What now, Hudson?" Duane asked.

"Chuck Smeller is here to see Buddy and Cassidy," he said. "He needs a word with them immediately."

"Can you tell Mr. Smeller that we're right in the middle of rehearsing the special?"

"I did, but he insisted that he was sent by his boss, the president of the network. He says it's vitally important."

"Ask him if it'll still be vitally important two hours from now." Duane's patience was wearing thin.

"Uh, Duane," I said in my most polite tone of voice. "Chuck Smeller is Barbara Daniel's chief assistant. He's so important that he speaks on two cell phones at once. I've seen it myself. I think we should meet with him and see what he wants."

"Fine," Duane said. "Buddy and Cassidy, you guys go outside and talk with Mr. Smelly."

"It's Smeller," I said. "With an E-R."

"I know his name, Buddy. I was just making a joke. Go talk to him, but make it quick. We've got to finish acts one and two today."

Cassidy and I followed Hudson through the darkness along the path of fluorescent tape to the heavy metal door of Stage 42. When we pushed it open, I was blinded by the light pouring from the California sun. Mr. Smeller was waiting for us, all smiles.

"Buddy! Cassidy! My two favorite television stars! I brought you each a special treat. Buddy, here's a big, ripe avocado for you . . . I know you love them. And Cassidy, a bag of Hershey's Kisses for you. But don't let your mom see."

"I'll hide them until tomorrow," Cassidy said. "My mom's not going to be here then."

"Your mother, missing a day on the set?" Mr. Smeller asked. "Must be some big emergency."

"Actually, it's a little-sister emergency. Eloise won't sleep over at Space Camp without my mom or dad. So my mom agreed to spend the night with her."

"Oh, isn't that lovely."

"That's not the word she uses," Cassidy said, tucking the chocolate into her back pocket. "She calls it a pain in the neck. Actually, she calls it a pain in another part of your body, but I'm not allowed to say the word."

"Oh, you mean a pain in the butt?" I chimed in. "I looked that up in my Earth slang dictionary. It listed a whole lot of other words for butt, like buttocks, rear end, rump and—"

"That's enough, Buddy. Mr. Smeller gets the picture."

Mr. Smeller let loose with a big, jolly laugh.

"No wonder you two are major stars," he said. "Look at the chemistry you've got between you. It's explosive."

"That sounds dangerous," I said. "Once I saw a meteor

explode and it was scary. It was a giant fireball that sent powerful shock waves across the universe."

Mr. Smeller laughed. "Always in character, Buddy. That's why you keep attracting all those fans who want to believe that you're really an alien. It's what people want to see. Which is exactly why I'm here."

"To talk about meteor explosions? I could do that all day long."

"Some other time, perhaps. I've come here to help your careers explode. We have a great opportunity. You two have been asked to do a special feature interview tomorrow for *Star Round-Up*."

"The talk show?" Cassidy said. "Wow. Everyone watches that."

"In this business we call show, it's known as must-see TV," Mr. Smeller said. "And we've got you booked on it!"

"What do we have to do?" I asked.

"The usual. Sit on a couch and talk to the host. Tell him how funny and exciting the show is. Be charming. Make easy conversation."

"And that would include not listing all your synonyms for butt," Cassidy added.

"Oh, I think people are always interested in expanding their vocabulary," I said.

"Listen to Cassidy, Buddy," Mr. Smeller said. "You two are supposed to be the wholesome new stars of television. So keep it clean, keep it fun, and most of all, say the name of the show a minimum of three times."

"I can do that," I said. "*Oddball Academy. Oddball Academy. Oddball Academy.*"

"I think it's better if you can spread that out over the conversation."

"The only bad thing is that we're doing camera rehearsals tomorrow," Cassidy said. "And Duane is really riding us hard."

"I've already taken care of that," Mr. Smeller said. "They're taping *Star Round-Up* on Stage 47. A quick golf-cart ride away. You'll be back on set within an hour. I'll come pick you up at noon tomorrow."

"My mom's going to be so sad to miss the taping. She loves that show. She watches it every day in my dressing room."

"She'll get over it," Mr. Smeller said. "Oh, excuse me, my pockets are ringing."

He pulled a cell phone out of each pocket and held one up to each ear.

"Smeller here," he said, turning his head from one phone to the other. "Oh yes, boss. No problem. The kids are all set for tomorrow. I had to have a little talk with Buddy, but he gets it now. Can you hold just a sec?"

Then speaking into the other phone, he said in a snappy voice, "No, she wanted dressing on the side. And no tomatoes. I'll pick it up in five minutes." He clicked off that call and his smile came back in an instant as he resumed talking to Barbara Daniel on the other phone.

"I'm on it, boss," he said. "One talk show, one salad, no tomatoes. You know me, I get the job done. Oh, excuse me, you *do* want tomatoes. That's what I was just about to tell them. Extra tomatoes."

He hung up the phone and jumped into his golf cart.

"Got to go, kids. You can't keep a chopped tomato waiting. I'll pick you up tomorrow. Until then, be great."

As Mr. Smeller sped off down the alley between two gigantic sound stages, my super-duper hearing could hear his left pocket ringing. Maybe his boss had changed her mind about the tomatoes again.

9

When we came back to rehearsal, everyone was curious about why Chuck Smeller had come to see us. Tyler was the most curious. I think he smelled that something was up. At our next break, I was sitting on the audience bleachers going over my lines when he slithered up to me like a snake about to strike. Helping himself to a seat, he flashed me his typical sneer.

"So, doofus," he said. "I presume Smeller came to offer some network suggestions on how you can look better."

"You're half right, Tyler. He did have suggestions."

"I knew it. It was about your muscle definition, wasn't it? No one wants to see flab, even on an alien. You have to work out, like me. You can't use my equipment, of course, but if you're nice, I'll tell you where I get it."

Cassidy and Luis came up to us, carrying four big cups

of water. I took one and drank it down in one gulp. Then I took the extra cups and drank those too.

"You must have a bladder like a camel," Tyler said. "If I drank that much water, I'd be peeing every ten minutes."

"We aliens love hydration," I said.

"Can you please knock off the alien thing for a minute," Tyler said. "There are no fans around to impress."

"Speaking of impressing people," Cassidy said, "did Buddy tell you about tomorrow?" She took two Hershey's Kisses out of her jeans pocket and popped one into her mouth, offering the other one to Tyler.

"No thanks," he said. "Chocolate is bad for my complexion. And what's this about tomorrow?"

"They've asked us to do an interview on *Star Round-Up* to promote the special."

Tyler's whole face lit up. "We are? Totally cool. I'll see if I can get my hair and makeup guy Bruce to come with me. Good thing I didn't eat that candy."

Tyler pulled his phone out of his jacket pocket, but Luis held up his hand to stop him.

"Slow down, chief," he said. "From what I hear, you didn't make the list."

"What would you know about anything?" Tyler said.

"I know that the total number of people on Earth who think you're great is one, and that one happens to be you."

"Howard Hitchcock certainly doesn't agree with you," Tyler said. "For your info, he called and wants me to join him in the commissary after rehearsal to start nailing down the details of our movie."

"That shows what he knows," Luis said.

Tyler ignored him. I mean, totally ignored him, as in he actually turned his back to him.

"Cassidy, he wants you to join us too, to see if you're right for the role of the fair maiden. But maybe I'll tell him you're too busy doing a third-rate talk show and your schedule doesn't allow it."

"Oh, Tyler, please don't tell him that," Cassidy said. "The talk show isn't until tomorrow. I'd love to meet with him after work. I'll go tell my mom."

"Your mom can come, but she has to sit in the corner and keep quiet," Tyler said. "You don't compete with Howard Hitchcock when he's discussing his creative ideas. He's a genius."

"Like you'd know a genius if you ran smack into one," Luis said. "By the way, Cassidly, if your mom does come, do you think it's even remotely possible that she keeps her lips zipped?"

"Lip zipping isn't exactly her specialty," I commented.

"But my mom wants to hear all my offers," Cassidy said.

"You have to show Mr. Hitchcock that you're your own person, that you can speak for yourself," Tyler said.

"I have an idea, Cass," I volunteered. "Delores told me that she was getting her nails done before she picks us up," I said. "I'll offer to go with her and get my nails trimmed too. Mine grow so fast that it will keep them busy until your meeting is over."

"That works out just fine," Tyler said. "Because Mr. Hitchcock did mention that he wants to see you too. But now I can tell him you're busy taking care of your extremely disgusting personal grooming needs."

"Buddy, I can't believe you're going miss a meeting with Howard Hitchcock just so I can go," Cassidy protested.

"That's okay, there's plenty of time for me to talk to him. You just go be brilliant and let me know when Delores and I should come get you."

Cassidy threw her arm around me. I think that's what you humans

93

would classify as a sort of hug. Hugs are a great thing you earthlings have invented, along with pizza, showers, and convertible cars.

"Buddy, you're the best friend ever," she said. My sensory enhancer got a whiff of the chocolate on her breath and let out a snort.

"Your costume's farting," Tyler said.

"It does that when it needs batteries," Cassidy answered. She's always ready at the drop of a hat to cover for me.

"Yeah," I said quickly. "I've got some double As in my dressing room. I gotta go."

I hurried off before my sensory enhancer could launch into a full-on snort fest. Away from the scent of chocolate, my enhancer calmed down, and within a few minutes, I was able to go back and take my place on the set.

We started to rehearse the next scene, which took place in the locker room. We were supposed to be hiding from the flying saucer by crouching under the benches while we tried to figure out an escape plan.

"Ulysses, I want you under the first bench," Duane said, "and Martha, you hide behind the open locker door."

"But I'm too tall to hide behind there," Martha said.

"Think small."

"I can't. I've got a big personality."

"Use your imagination. That's what acting is all about."

I could see Martha trying to shrivel up by folding her arms and raising her shoulders to shorten her neck. It looked painful, and you could still see her left side sticking out from behind the locker.

"Just do your best," Duane said. "Buddy, I want you at the window, looking out to track the movements of the flying saucer. You should take a beat, then react when you see the first alien walking down the ramp."

I followed his direction and looked out the window. Then I improvised a line.

"Hi, guys," I said, waving my seven-fingered hand. "Come on in and make yourselves home."

"Cut! Cut! Cut!" Duane hollered, springing from his director's chair. "That's not in the script. You're supposed to be terrified of the aliens."

"Why?"

"Because they're aliens, invading Earth."

"Maybe they're friendly and just stopped in for a smoothie?"

"Everyone knows that when aliens come to Earth, they're here to conquer us and not to drink fruity beverages."

"I think that's very narrow minded of you," I said. "Aliens could be coming here to help us. To teach us how to give up using plastic or clean up the air so we can breathe better."

Ulysses immediately went into his imitation of an alien voice.

"We have come to rescue you from yourselves, earthlings. Switch to electric vehicles and your nostrils will enjoy clean air. All for the low price of twenty-nine thousand dollars. If you order two, you get free shipping."

We were laughing so hard that at first we didn't notice the flapping sound coming from the back of the sound stage. But when we saw Howard Hitchcock's parrot emerge out of the darkness and swoop down onto our set, we couldn't believe our eyes. Squawking up a storm, it landed on the open locker door where Martha was crouched.

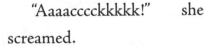

"Aaaacccckkkkk!" she screamed.

The bird lifted its tail feathers and deposited a goopy, white splotch on Martha's head.

Her "aaaccckkk" changed to an "eeeuuuww," and I can't

say I blamed her. No matter what planet you're from, having bird poop on your head is totally gross.

"Someone call Mr. Hitchcock and tell him Zelda got loose," I said.

"*Squawk!* Shut up your tongues! *Squawk!*"

Did that bird say tongues, with an "s"? Did it know that I actually do have two tongues? Or did it just have a lisp?

"Follow me," Zelda ordered. "Now! *Squawk!*"

"Who does your boss want to see?" Tyler asked.

"You! You!" Zelda pointed her feathered wing at Tyler and Cassidy, and then turned directly to me. "Him too! *Squawk!*"

"Listen, Zelda, or whatever your bird name is," Duane said, walking up to the bird and folding his arms in a determined stance. "We are in a time crunch here, and I can't just be sending my cast out on film interviews whenever your boss snaps his fingers. And I can't believe I'm having this conversation with a bird."

"But Duane," Tyler protested. "This is my future. My big shot."

"And mine too," Cassidy said, a little more softly.

"I'm sorry, you two, but I . . ."

I could see Duane was about to tell them both that they couldn't leave, so I jumped in quickly.

"Hey, Duane, we only have an hour left anyway. And Luis and I need to go over our dialogue with Martha and Ulysses. So we really don't need Tyler and Cassidy. We could just let them knock off early."

Duane looked at his watch and thought for a minute.

"Okay," he sighed. "I guess they can go meet with that fashion freak. Cassidy and Tyler, just be sure you are well acquainted with act three so we can hit the ground running tomorrow."

"Thanks, loser! *Squawk!*" the parrot cackled.

We all looked at one another in amazement. No one talks to Duane like that.

"Hey, little birdie," Luis said, without hesitation. "This dude is the boss in chief. He deserves respect. Take that back."

"Take it back, loser!" Zelda squawked, flying off toward the stage door before Duane could tell her what he really thought of her.

"Good luck," I whispered to Cassidy as Tyler followed Zelda to the door.

"I plan to knock Mr. Hitchcock's socks off," Cassidy whispered back.

"Oh, don't do that. His boots will rub blisters all over his heels."

"It's an expression, Buddy. I'll explain it later."

"I look forward to that. In the meantime, just believe in yourself as much as I believe in you. You're going to be great."

I rolled all six of my eyes around to the front so she could look in every one of them and see the confidence I had in her.

And then she went after Tyler and Zelda.

The rest of us got involved in rehearsing the scene, and it went really well. Luis was getting the hang of it, and Martha added a funny song about how cool aliens are. The title was "I'm Hip, I'm Here, and I'm Alien." It had a good beat.

When Delores came to pick us up, she was surprised that Cassidy wasn't there.

"She and Tyler were called into a sudden meeting with Mr. Hitchcock," I explained, crawling into the front seat of her car.

"Without me?" Delores couldn't believe her ears.

"I'm sure you'll be invited to the next meeting." I explained.

"It can't be tomorrow, Mommy," Eloise said from the back seat. "Don't forget, you're going to Space Camp with me."

"I keep trying to forget, but unfortunately, the horrible

reality won't go away." Delores shuddered. "I'm seeing a bunk in my future."

"Thank goodness we have manicure appointments now to help blot out the thought," I said, trying to be my most cheerful self.

"But you're still in your costume," Eloise said.

"That's okay. Even costumes need manicures. Especially mine."

"Well, I'm going to get a fruit cocktail," Eloise giggled.

"They don't serve fruit at manicure parlors," Delores said.

"No, Mommy. A fruit cocktail on my nails. Each nail is going to be a different color of fruit. Apple red. Mango orange. Pineapple yellow. Plum purple. Green grape."

"Okay, okay, I get it, Eloise. You don't have to name every fruit in the world. You've only got ten fingers."

"But my costume has fourteen," I said to Eloise. "So keep coming up with fruits."

"They're going to have enough to do just to get your nails cut. They're gross."

"They're excellent for scratching your back in those hard-to-reach places."

"That's even grosser," Eloise moaned.

I looked out the window as we wove our way across the lot to the main gate.

"Cassidy said she'll call as soon as the interview is over," I told Delores, "and we can come back and pick her up."

"Was she nervous?" Delores asked. "I hope not. She always chews on her lower lip when she's nervous and that is very unpleasant looking."

"She looked confident," I said. "No lip chewing involved. I gave her a good pep talk, just like you would have."

"Good," Delores said. "I hope she remembered to put on some blusher. And to keep away from those Hershey's Kisses I saw stashed in her makeup drawer."

"Mom, you go in her makeup drawer?" Eloise asked.

"Of course. A mother's job is never done."

"Have you been in mine?"

"You don't have a makeup drawer, Eloise, you're seven. But I am aware you hide purple unicorn gummies in between your socks. You better stop that, missy, unless you want your toes to stick together for ever and ever."

I looked into the back seat and saw Eloise's eyes grow wide with fear as she reached down to her feet and pulled off her shoes to wiggle her toes.

"I don't actually think it would be forever," I whispered. "Maybe just for a few months until the candy disintegrates."

She relaxed when she saw her toes were still free. Poor little thing. It's hard to be seven.

When we reached Lanny's Nail Salon, we were put into massage chairs that vibrated when you sat in them. I'm not sure what the point of that is, but Delores let out a loud sigh when she plopped herself down, so I assume constant jiggling is something you humans enjoy. We all soaked our hands in hot lemon water and that did feel truly great. My nails must have loved it because they started to curl into beautiful shapes.

The manicure was a wonderful distraction and Delores hardly mentioned Cassidy's interview with Mr. Hitchcock. Instead, she spent the whole time analyzing all the different shades of red and trying to decide which one had the most "pop." I'm not sure why fingernails need to pop, but it was very important to Delores.

I got at least three inches trimmed off my nails, but by the time Cassidy called, they were already starting to grow back. On my planet, keeping our fingernails short enough so we don't poke ourselves to death is pretty much a full-time job. We all have special nail clippers hanging from our belts, and we have citizens whose only job is to sweep up the nail clippings from the streets. I don't want to gross you out, but one year I kept all of my nail clippings in a jar just to see how much my body produced. I collected enough to fill a large tub of your movie popcorn.

No butter, of course.

"Hey Cass," I said into the phone. "We're almost done here."

"I'm ready to be picked up," she said. "I'll be waiting at the studio front gate."

"How was it?" I couldn't wait to hear all the details.

"Out of this world," was all she said, hanging up.

With Delores waving her hands in the air to help dry her nails, and Eloise chattering about red bananas and pink limes, we got back in the car and drove the few blocks down Ventura Blvd to the studio. Just like she promised, Cassidy was waiting at the front gate.

"What took you so long?" she said as she climbed into the back seat next to Eloise. "You don't keep a star waiting."

I laughed, thinking it was a joke, but Cassidy didn't smile. Instead she grumbled at Eloise, "Move your hairy leg out of my way. You're hogging the whole back seat."

"Somebody is a rotten mood," Eloise said. "And my legs aren't hairy."

"Don't talk back to me," Cassidy said. "Just do what I say."

I rotated all my eyes to the back so I could get a good look at Cassidy. Something was going on with her, but I couldn't tell what. What I saw in her eyes was a blank look. I had never seen that look before, and I didn't like it.

Not one bit.

10

When we pulled into the driveway, Cassidy got out of the car almost before it stopped moving.

"I'm going to my room," she said.

"No you're not." Delores jumped out of the driver's seat so fast that it seemed like her pants were on fire.

"Mom, you can't tell me what to do," Cassidy said.

"Actually, I can and I will, young lady. It's my job. You're going to come inside, sit down at the kitchen table, and tell me every detail of what happened in your meeting with Howard Hitchcock. And you're going to knock off the sour attitude."

"I'm all for that," Eloise chimed in. "Cassidy's face looks like she sucked on a lemon."

"Buddy," Delores said as she rummaged through her huge purse for the house keys. "Why don't you quickly change out of your costume before you join us in the kitchen."

"I'm all for that too," Eloise said. "No offense, Buddy, but you smell like belly button lint."

"That doesn't sound so bad," I said. "Lint is soft and fresh."

"Not yours," Cassidy snapped.

I decided to ignore that comment and give Cassidy a chance to get back into her usual good mood. I went into my room, sat on the bed, and took my amulet from around my neck and held it in the palm of my hand. Closing my fingers around it to feel its warmth and power, I shut my eyes and began to chant.

"*Be Zane now*," I said softly, over and over again. "*Be Zane Tracy.*"

My biological alteration powers were in great form, because I could immediately feel the transformation from alien to human begin. My bald scalp sprouted a thick head of human hair, my alien eyeballs collapsed into just two human eyes, my seven fingers took the shape of human hands, and my cobalt-blue skin became completely human and encased my sensory enhancer. The only thing left was to convert my suction cup toes into human feet. For some reason, that part of the transformation seemed to stall.

"*Be Zane now, and I'm talking toes too*," I chanted,

holding the amulet a little tighter. "Come on feet, you can do it."

My incantation worked because within seconds, my suction cups receded back into my feet and five adorable human toes emerged on each foot. Even though I've been on this planet for almost two months, I still have great admiration for your earthling toes. They don't do much but they're fun to look at and they wiggle.

When I entered the kitchen, Eloise was counting all the doughnuts that were in a box on the kitchen counter.

"There are six chocolate, three sprinkles, and three glazed." She grinned when she saw me. "They're going to be a surprise for my bunkmates. And they're delicious."

"How do you know?" I asked her.

"I tore off a crumb from each one of them," she said. "You have to look very hard to notice."

Delores was on her phone confirming the final arrangements for our interview with *Star Round-Up* the next day. Whoever the other person was on the phone, they didn't get a chance to say much. Delores was in full manager mode.

"Now, make sure that Cassidy isn't lit from above because I don't want to see shadows on her cheeks. And on her last interview she had on way too much blush. It made her look like she was auditioning for the circus. And will there be a seamstress in case her skirt needs to be shortened? We want to see knee but not thigh. And made sure she sits up straight in the chair so no belly comes over the skirt."

"Mom," Cassidy barked. "Can you knock it off? My belly is my business."

"Don't get so touchy," Delores said. "This is all for your own good. That interview is going to be seen by the whole country."

Delores ended the conversation with one last round of instructions and ended the call.

"I don't know where you'd be without me," she said. "Probably still trying out for a bit part in the school play."

"I'm so way beyond that, Mom. I have unmistakable star quality, and I didn't make that up myself. Howard Hitchcock said my star is just beginning to shine and the entire universe awaits me."

"Take it from me, the entire universe is pretty big," I commented. "That Mr. Hitchcock certainly has big hopes for you."

"It's not a hope, Buddy, it's a reality. He says I'm going to redefine greatness."

Cassidy got up from the kitchen table and went to the refrigerator to pour herself a cold glass of water.

"I'll have one of those," I said. "You know me and water . . . I can't get enough of it."

"Get it yourself," Cassidy said. "I'm not here to wait on you."

"Hey, I just thought as long as you were there . . ."

"Buddy, we have to redefine our relationship. From now on, you have to do more for me than I do for you."

Delores looked up from her phone and actually did something I'd never seen her do before. She put it down. "You're getting way too big for your britches, Cassidy," she said sternly. "And I'm not talking about your butt."

"Oh, that's a first."

"There's an example," Delores said. "That tone of voice is unacceptable. I don't know what Mr. Hitchcock has filled your head with, but you need to empty it out. Greatness takes work. You don't just talk about it and assume you're the world's biggest star. You have to earn that. And put down that doughnut."

"I'll put it down, all right," Cassidy said. She took the whole box of doughnuts from the countertop, tossed them all into the sink, and turned on the water.

"No!" Eloise burst into tears. "Those were a special treat for my bunkmates."

She ran to the sink and pulled herself up so she could

reach the water faucet to turn it off. She yanked off several sheets of paper towels and tried desperately to dry off as many of the doughnuts as she could.

"This isn't working," she cried. "They're all soggy. And those are the good ones. The others have turned to mush already."

"Cassidy, you're out of control," her mother said. "Apologize to your sister, then go to your room. Think about your attitude and make a personality correction, because I don't know this person who is standing in front of me right now."

"It's me, Mom. Get used to it." Cassidy turned to Eloise. "Sorry about your greasy doughnuts, kiddo. They would have gotten stale by tomorrow anyway."

With that nonapology, Cassidy stomped out of the kitchen, down the hall into her room, and slammed the door.

"I'm getting a bad feeling about this Howard Hitchcock," Delores said. "He's filling her head with that haughty attitude, and believe you me, the audience will pick up on that right away. Arrogance turns people off faster than they can change the channel. I've seen careers crash and burn in a nanosecond."

Poor little Eloise was still trying to piece together the remains of the doughnuts.

"If I put the chocolate one and the sprinkles one together with the pink one, it almost makes a whole doughnut," she said. She used her fingers to try to connect the three by smoothing frosting over the cracks. When she picked it up, all the doughnuts crumbled onto the floor in a soggy mess at her feet. She burst into tears again.

"Stupid Cassidy," she sobbed. "Why did she have to ruin everything?" Then she ran down the hall to her room and slammed the door.

"There's a lot of door slamming going on tonight," I said, trying to lighten the mood.

"Maybe you can help, Buddy," Delores said. "You have a very soothing way of talking to Cassidy. Why don't you give it try."

"Okay," I said. "I'll go down to her room, and I promise I won't slam the door."

"I'm going to pack," Delores said. "I wonder what kind of clothes a person needs for Space Camp."

"I'd suggest a little less jewelry than you usually wear," I offered. "You don't want your bracelets and rings to get caught up in the control panel, which would interfere with your interplanetary navigation."

Delores laughed. "Sometimes, Buddy, you actually have me believing you are a space alien."

I laughed too, a little too loud and a little too long.

I left the kitchen and headed to Cassidy's room. I hesitated before I knocked on her door. Just between you and me, I was a little nervous. I'm not good at dealing with your human emotions, and I had a feeling there were a lot of big ones waiting for me on the other side of that door.

"Knock, knock," I said, instead of actually knocking. I thought it sounded friendlier, but I found out immediately how wrong I was.

"Leave me alone," Cassidy shouted.

"I just want to talk for a minute."

"I definitely do not want to talk, and especially not to you!"

"Hey, Cass, do you remember who's out here in the hall? It's me, your good friend Buddy. Your acting partner. Your pal." Then, lowering my voice to a whisper, I added, "Your best alien friend in the whole universe."

I heard footsteps and the door to her room flew open so fast it created a gust of wind that blew my human hair straight up in the air. Cassidy was holding her phone and obviously in the middle of a conversation. She pointed to the phone as if to say, "Can't you see I'm on the phone."

"I'll wait," I mouthed.

"Okay, but don't say a word."

She gestured for me to come in and turned her back on me to continue her phone conversation.

"It's no one, Mr. Hitchcock," she said into the phone. "Just Buddy Burger. Oh, really? Why would you want to talk to him?"

"Maybe he sees my star potential too," I whispered.

"Don't be ridiculous," she whispered back. "He's not stupid. He knows real talent when he sees it."

That made me feel like I was about two inches tall. What happened to Cassidy, my good friend who supported me no matter what? Obviously, she wasn't living at this address.

"Thank you so much for calling, Mr. Hitchcock," Cassidy said, flopping down on her desk chair. "I'll remember all the tips you gave me for the talk show appearance tomorrow. I'll seize my moment like you told me and introduce America to a brand-new me."

She hung up the phone and flashed me a big smile. There she was, my old friend, with a smile that could light up the universe.

"That was good," she said. "Mr. Hitchcock just told me he's going to be my new mentor. How lucky can a person get?"

"So how about sharing his tips with me, so I can be good on the talk show, too?" I asked.

"Okay, here's a tip. Get out of my room."

"Wow, he said that?"

"No, dumbbell. I said that."

Maybe I was a little too quick to think my friend had returned. She wasted no time in getting me out of there.

"Thanks for the visit, Buddy, but I need to be alone now to prepare."

"For what?"

"My future life that starts now."

"Fine, I'm here. Let's talk about it. I'm part of your future life too."

"Frankly, Buddy, I'm not interested in anything you have to say. From now on, I'm only listening to Mr. Hitchcock. He has my best interests at heart."

"Are you sure?"

"Of course I'm sure. And I resent you even questioning that. You're just jealous, and trust me, jealousy doesn't look good on you. Especially coming out of six eyes."

"I thought you liked my alien eyes?"

"That was yesterday—this is today. I'm just not into bald blue aliens anymore."

That was certainly a conversation ender. I went through my whole catalog of human responses and I couldn't come up with anything to say, so I left.

Back in my room, I could feel my energy dwindling down to almost nothing. I didn't know if it was from the conversation or from the end of a long day at the studio, but the combination was more than I could take. I felt like overcooked spaghetti that just lies there on the bottom of the pot. I needed to get into the bath with no time to spare.

I turned on the water in my tub, climbed out of my jeans and T-shirt, and plunged in. As I soaked in the tub, I felt a wave of sadness come over me. Cassidy was such a major part of my happiness on Earth and now suddenly, I was no one to her. I felt like I didn't know her anymore. Why was she acting this way? I hadn't done anything different. I was just me.

As my mind cleared and grew stronger, I realized that the one

different thing that had happened to Cassidy was the meeting with Mr. Hitchcock. He was the one who put the idea of stardom in her head. He was the one who changed her.

I made up my mind right then and there that if I got a chance to meet with him, I was going to ask him exactly what he had said to Cassidy that changed her entire personality. Whoever this guy was, he had a lot of power over people. From watching the Supreme Leader take over my planet, I know that having absolute power is not a good thing. It takes away people's ability to be themselves.

I felt like that's what was happening to Cassidy. Her old self was disappearing, and I sure didn't like the new one.

11

*T**he next morning, I woke up feeling hopeful that*** the new day would bring the old Cassidy back. When I strolled into the kitchen for my breakfast avocado, she was standing at the stove, scrambling eggs fiercely, like she was angry at them. Egg yolk was flying all over the place and she was yelling at the poor, helpless eggs.

"Hurry up and cook," she barked. "And don't look at me with your goopy orange eyes."

"I hope the eggs aren't answering you," I said.

"Buddy, that would be even weirder than you," Eloise said. She had several purple and yellow Froot Loops stuck above her upper lip. I couldn't tell if she had put them there on purpose or if was an accident. Either way, it was pretty cute.

Delores came clomping into the kitchen, and I do mean clomping. She was wearing her idea of space boots, which had clunky heels that were at least three inches tall, fur linings, and bright, shiny, purple leather up to her knees. Cassidy shot her a look that was the very definition of disapproving.

"Mom," she groaned. "What is that going on with your feet?"

"Space boots. Haven't you ever seen pictures of astronauts? They all wear boots."

"Not like those, Mom," Cassidy said. "If you wear those, someone's going to call the fashion police and give you a ticket for footwear violation."

"I'm just trying to put some fun into this Space Camp thing," Delores said. "School field trips are not my cup of tea."

"Maybe you should try coffee instead," I suggested. It seemed like a reasonable idea if she didn't like tea, but Delores was not open to the suggestion.

"I hope you don't make corny jokes like that on your talk show appearance today," she snapped. "You're there to sell the special to the audience, and you need to focus. Repeat the title at least three times so the audience will remember to tune in. You got that?"

"We know what to do, Mom," Cassidy said, shoveling all the eggs on a plate for herself. She didn't offer me any, which wasn't like her, because she's usually a big-time sharer.

"Luis should be here any minute to pick you guys up and take you to the studio," Delores said, looking at her watch, which had enough dials on it to actually navigate her through outer space. "I'll call throughout the day to check in."

"No you won't," Eloise said. "There's no phones allowed at Space Camp."

"I'm not a camper, Eloise. Besides, my phone is permanently connected to my ear. It would have to be medically removed, and then I couldn't take you to camp."

I heard Luis's car pull up in the driveway. His car, which he calls Muriel, is his prized possession. It's a red convertible, which I love to ride in when the top is down. My human hair blows all over my face and tickles my nose, which makes me sneeze and is really a lot of fun. On my planet, there is no such thing as a nose sneeze. During a red dust storm, we all wear *snorks*, which are nostril shields. They protect our noses and force us to sneeze through our ears. That gets messy, and trust me, you don't want to know the details. Let's just it involves green particles spewing out your ears. I'm not even going to mention the yellow ones.

Luis tooted his horn and hollered for us.

"Your chariot has arrived," he called. "All aboard for Universal Studios."

"Time for us to go," I said, grabbing my pack and throwing it on my back. I heard my sensory enhancer grunt.

"Did you just fart?" Eloise said.

"Of course not. I was just clearing my throat through my back."

Eloise burst out laughing and Delores shot me a stern look.

"None of your space jokes during your interview. Remember why you're there. Be charming, not weird."

"When was the last time that happened?" Cassidy muttered as she impatiently stuffed her script and water bottle into her messenger bag.

"Have a great time in space, you guys," I said, giving Eloise's pigtails a playful tug.

"I'll bring you something from Mars, Buddy. Maybe a red rock."

"I'd like that. I haven't been to Mars in a long time."

Luis tooted his horn again. "We're going to be late," he shouted. "I don't want to hear about it from Duane, so step on it."

"Why do you always have to be so loud?" Cassidy complained as she climbed into the front seat.

"And good morning to you," Luis answered. "You got a case of the grouchies?"

"Mind your own business," Cassidy snapped. "My mood belongs to me, and it's not a topic of discussion."

"I think, Cass, you should sit in the back," I suggested. "Maybe you need some quiet time."

"Fine, I need to make a call to Mr. Hitchcock anyway."

"Whoa, you and the Big Man are getting really tight, I see," Luis said.

"He has become my career guru."

"Overnight?" Luis said. "Wow, that was fast."

"Talent waits for no one. Now if you'll just drive, I have a call to make."

As Luis backed down the driveway, he shot a glance at me.

"What's up with her?" he whispered.

"I think it's Hitchcock," I whispered back.

"I'm right here," Cassidy said from the back seat. "I can hear every word. I'm not invisible."

"We'll talk later," I mouthed to Luis. We turned on the radio and drove the rest of the way to Universal Studios without a word.

When we pulled up to Stage 42, Chuck Smeller was sitting in a golf cart by the stage door. Naturally, he was on both of his phones. I have never seen anyone with busier ears.

"Top of the morning," he said, dropping a phone into each of his coat pockets at once. "You guys ready for the interview?"

"Right now?" I said.

"Yup."

"We have to go tell Duane that we're going to miss some rehearsal time."

"Handled!" he said. "Just got off the phone with him. I told him I'd have you back on set in an hour."

"Was he mad?"

"Yes, but when I told him this was an order from my boss, Barbara Daniel, he collapsed like a popped balloon."

"The publicity will be really good for our show," Luis said.

Chuck Smeller looked him up and down.

"And who exactly are you?" he asked.

"That's Luis Rivera," I said proudly. "He's our guest star this week."

"Oh, suddenly he's the star," Cassidy snapped. "I thought I was the star."

"Of course you are, young lady," Mr. Smeller said. "That's why you're doing the talk show. Come on, let's get you guys in makeup." Then turning to Luis, he added, "Nice meeting you . . . what's your name again?"

"Luis Rivera."

"Of course it is. I'll put you in my contacts list, in case you hit it big."

We got out of the car and Luis drove off to find a space

in the actors' parking lot. Cassidy sat in the front of the golf cart next to Smeller, and I rode in back. Lots of people waved to me and we drove through the narrow lanes between sound stages. It was nice to know they recognized me even without my alien costume.

Costume? What am I saying? It's not a costume, it's me. Am I starting to believe my own story?

Barbara Daniel was waiting for us outside the door to Stage 47.

"Hey, boss," Mr. Smeller said, plastering on an insincere grin that stretched across his whole lower face. "I got your stars right here, safe and sound."

"They only work five sound stages over, Chuck," she said. "It's not like you're Magellan circumnavigating the globe."

"I don't know, it got pretty hairy over there by the Hitchcock stage. We got stuck behind a tram full of tourists who were all taking pictures of Cassidy and Buddy."

"They are so annoying, those fans. I've had it with them." Cassidy said.

"Remember, those are the paying customers who keep you on the air," Ms. Daniel pointed out. She said it with a smile, but it was definitely a reprimand.

"We love our fans," I said, "don't we, Cass?" I looked at her face, and it was still as blank as an empty piece of paper. I tried again. "We never forgot how lucky we are, right, Cass?" Still nothing. It was a long silence until she finally spoke.

"Can you just show me where my dressing room is?" she said. "And I hope there's cold water, a cheese tray . . . not those annoying cheddar cubes . . . and chocolate-covered pretzels."

"If there isn't, I will take care of it right away," Chuck Smeller said, taking one of the phones from his pocket and opening the door to the sound stage with his other hand.

"Hello, Bea. Ix-nay on the eddar-chay," he whispered into the phone. "Oh, sorry. You don't speak Pig Latin? I'll translate. Get rid of the cheddar cubes. Pronto. Oh, you don't speak Italian, either? That means right away."

He flashed another of his fake grins, and I noticed Barbara Daniel shaking her head and sighing deeply.

"You kids go and get into makeup," she said. "I'll meet you on the stage and introduce you to your interviewer, Linda Chen. Oh, and Buddy, I hope you brought your costume. It'd be good for you to appear as the alien."

"No problem, Ms. Daniel. I have it with me."

"Where? I don't see it."

Oops. I looked over at Cassidy, who usually helps me out when I'm caught in a situation like this. But she just stared at me.

"Why are you looking at me?" she snapped.

"Uh, no reason. I just thought maybe knew where my costume is."

"I'm not your costume carrier, Buddy."

"Of course not. Anyway, I have it right here in my pocket. It folds up very small."

"What an amazing piece of technology," Ms. Daniel said. "I never get over movie magic."

"Me either. I'll go to my dressing room and put it on right now."

"Wonderful. The dressing rooms on the Hitchcock stage are lovely. Alfred Hitchcock had a special one designed just for him that looked like his library at home."

"I'll take that one," Cassidy said. "After all, I'm practically part of the Hitchcock family."

We all walked into the sound stage. The crew and camera operators were on a coffee break, helping themselves to snacks at the craft service table. Down on the set, I saw Linda Chen going over her notes with the producer.

"Make yourselves look great," Ms. Daniel said. "Meet you back here in ten minutes."

The stage manager, who introduced himself as Mel and wore a baseball cap backward under his headset, showed us to our dressing rooms. Cassidy got the Alfred Hitchcock one. I noticed that there was a tray of cheese and crackers sitting on the long, shiny mahogany table. Unfortunately for Mr. Smeller, it was cheddar cubes. Cassidy glared at them.

"I specifically requested no cheddar, and no toothpicks," she said to Mel.

"They're bringing you a new tray right now, miss," he answered. "It's coming from the commissary."

"It's about time," she snapped. "Can you leave now? I need to be alone to speak with my mentor."

Mel took me to my dressing room next door. For some reason, it was decorated like a ski lodge in Switzerland. There was a pair of skis hung crisscrossed on the wall and a huge painting of the Alps that seemed so real, it almost made me feel cold.

"Your makeup person will be here in a few minutes," Mel said. "Anything I can get you while you wait?"

"I'm going to change into my costume," I said, "so I need a little privacy."

"Should I send a wardrobe person to press out the wrinkles?"

"No thanks, they press themselves out. My costume is pretty skintight."

After he left and closed the door, I sat down on a fake fur blanket that was tossed on a rustic chair made of pine logs. The fur tickled my rear end and I let out a little laugh. Once my enhancer was out in the open, I knew it was going to love that texture. I hoped I could stop it from giggling. Closing my eyes, I held my amulet and began my biological alteration.

"*Be the real me,*" I chanted. "*Be the real me now.*"

I was on my game, and within seconds, my alien body emerged. Just as I feared, my sensory enhancer dove into the fake fur and burrowed itself deep into the blanket. It snorted with pleasure and started to giggle. What I wasn't prepared for was the sneeze attack that followed. It was so strong that the force of the sneezes literally pushed me out of the chair and onto my feet. I heard a knock at the door.

"You need some tissues in there?" Mel called. "There's a box in the bathroom. Actually, there's two. Sounds like you might need them both."

"Just my nerves acting up," I called back. "I sneeze when I get nervous. I've never done a talk show before."

"You're going to crush it, dude," Mel said. "You ready for the sound person to put your mic on?"

"The question is, are you ready?" I whispered over my shoulder to my sensory enhancer. It sniffled softly, which told me that the sneeze fest was over. I opened the door, and smiled at Mel, giving him a good look at my red gums in all their glory. He did a double take. Maybe even a triple take.

"Whoa!" he said. "That costume really comes alive in the flesh. I wasn't prepared for it to look so real."

"Movie magic," I said.

"Want me to hang up your regular clothes?" he asked.

"Oh, that won't be necessary. I folded them and put them on the chair. They seem very happy there."

"You're so helpful, Buddy, not like your partner next door," Mel said. "Just between us, she's kicking up quite a fuss. Didn't like the replacement cheese, didn't find the water cold enough, didn't like the garlic breath on the makeup person, wouldn't let the hair stylist touch her curls. Is she always this difficult?"

"She never used to be," I said. "She's getting a lot of attention from a certain big-time director and it's kind of gone to her head. But promise not to say I said so."

"This is between you and me," Mel said. "I would get in a lot of trouble if anyone knew we had this conversation."

The door to Cassidy's dressing room flew open, and she came stomping out.

"Well, if it isn't Buddy the alien," she said. "Mr. Red Gums. And what is going on with your sensory enhancer? Tell me that's not snot."

I shot a glance at my sensory enhancer, and she had a point. There were some remains of the sneeze attack hanging off it.

"It's probably just some dip from the vegetable plate," I said. I didn't want Cassidy to even consider that it was snot, in case she decided to bring it up in the interview. The audience might never recover.

"Okay, guys," Mel said. "Follow me. I'll introduce you to Linda and then it's showtime."

As we walked down the hall and onto the set, I kept a close eye on Cassidy, trying to judge her mood. I hoped that it was better. All of America would be watching us, and I had no idea which Cassidy was going to appear . . . the charming girl who's my best friend or the self-important stranger who's mean to everyone.

All I could do was hope that the real Cassidy would show up.

12

m **el took us to the set and introduced us to** the host, Linda Chen, who was deep in conversation with Barbara Daniel. Ms. Daniel was describing our special and the high hopes the network had for it, while Linda nodded and looked over a set of large blue index cards with her questions on them. She looked up when we approached and welcomed us with a warm smile.

"Hi, Cassidy. Hi, Buddy. It's so good to have you on *Star Roundup*," she said. "Our audience is going to be thrilled to meet you. Love your costume, Buddy."

Before I could even say thank you, Cassidy piped up. "What about my outfit? His is the same every day. Mine was hand chosen just for this show. It took me an hour to decide which top to wear."

"Well, you certainly chose the right one," Linda said. "You look good in red."

"You don't have to tell me. Red is my power color."

There was an uncomfortable moment when we all stood there in silence, until Mel cleared his throat and changed the subject.

"Let me show you where you're going to sit for the interview," he said.

"Let me take a wild guess," Cassidy answered. "On the couch."

"Good guess," he said, ignoring her sarcastic tone. We followed his directions and sat down next to each other on the couch.

"Buddy, you sit here next to Linda, and Cassidy, you sit next to him," Mel directed. Then speaking into his headset, he said, "Control room, how does it look on camera? Okay, I'll move her farther down on the couch."

He gestured to Cassidy that she should slide a few inches away from me.

"Why do I have to move?" she asked.

"We need some separation between you and Buddy, so the camera can get a clear close-up of each of you."

"Close-ups are great," she said. "Especially when you look like me. Most actors have a good side and a bad side, but I happen to have two perfect sides,"

"Yes, you do," Mel said. "I can see that."

Boy, this guy must be used to working with demanding people, I thought. Cassidy was being totally impossible, but nothing seemed to remove the smile on his face. Even what happened next.

"I should sit next to Linda," Cassidy pouted. "I'll be doing most of the talking, and I should be in the number one seat."

She practically picked me up under the armpits to shove me farther down on the couch.

"Remember, kids, we want to hear from both of you," Ms. Daniel said, looking more at Cassidy than at me. "Each of you will have your close-ups, so it doesn't matter where you sit."

"It matters to me," Cassidy said.

Suddenly her phone, which was in the back pocket of her jeans, rang. I noticed she had changed her usual ring tone. It used to be the theme song of our show, but now it was someone singing a song called "I Will Always Love Me." I couldn't believe she answered it just as we were getting our final instructions about the interview.

"Hello," Cassidy said. "Yes, Mr. Hitchcock. Thanks for the reminder. Don't worry, I've got this. You can depend on me. I'll check in with you afterward."

She hung up as if she hadn't been keeping all of us waiting.

"What did he say?" I asked her.

"Nothing that would concern you."

That certainly put me in my place.

"We've got one minute before we start," Mel said. "Everybody relax and have a good time. Here's a cup of water for each of you."

He placed two mugs with the show's logo on the coffee table in front of us.

"Do we get to keep this?" I asked Mel.

"Yup, and you also will get a tee shirt with Linda's picture on it."

All of a sudden, I missed Grandma Wrinkle like crazy. If she could see me with my very own *Star Roundup* mug and tee shirt, she would be so happy. Everything we ever dreamed about was coming true for me.

"Oh, Mel," Cassidy said. "I can't use this mug. It's got to be cleaned in front of me. I don't know where it's been."

From out of nowhere, Chuck Smeller bounded onto the set. He pulled his handkerchief from his jacket pocket, shook it open with a flourish, and proceeded to wipe down the mug.

"My hankie and I are always happy to be of service," he said.

"I don't know where your hankie has been either," Cassidy said. "You're really not helping."

"We're live in five seconds," Mel called. "Five, four, three . . ."

Ms. Daniel extended an arm and yanked Chuck Smeller off the set, putting an end to his accidental television debut. Linda Chen plastered a big smile on her face and looked directly into the camera. She had great teeth. I took a deep breath to calm my fluttering stomachs, and Cassidy flipped her hair over her shoulder and shoved me a little farther down the couch.

"This is exciting," I whispered to her.

"I'm ready for my close-up," she said. "Never been so ready for anything in my life."

The red lights on the camera started to blink and just like that, we were live in millions of homes across the country.

"Good morning, America," Linda Chen began. "We have an exciting show today. Two of your favorite TV stars are here to give us an exclusive preview of the *Oddball Academy* special that airs this Friday. Buddy Burger and Cassidy Cambridge, welcome to *Star Roundup*."

I looked right into the camera and waved.

"Hi, everyone? Can you see me? This is my very first talk show ever."

Cassidy pushed her face in front of mine and flipped her hair in my face.

"Hi all you Cassidy fans out there," she said.

"Buddy, I know you get a lot of fan mail from kids who love that thing on your back," Linda began. "What is it called, and can you show us how it works?"

"It's called a sensory enhancer. It likes to smell strong scents," I said. "Cassidy, do you have a breath mint?"

"Of course I don't. My breath is as fresh as a daisy."

"How about coffee," Linda said. "I have a nice steaming cup right here."

I took the cup from Linda's hand and held it out so my sensory enhancer could take a good whiff. I knew I was taking a chance that it would go crazy, but with the cameras rolling and all of America tuned in, I couldn't let them down.

"Just a little sniff," I whispered over my shoulder.

When my sensory enhancer smelled the coffee, it let out

a squeal of delight and before I could stop it, it plunged its snout into the cup and took a big slurp.

Linda burst out laughing. "Look at that! Control room, are you getting a close-up? Buddy can make his costume come alive, and we don't even know how he's doing it."

My sensory enhancer started blowing bubbles in the coffee cup. Uh oh. What if it decided to spit out the coffee when it came up for air? It might spray Linda in the face. I couldn't let that happen. I gently took the cup away, grabbed my sensory enhancer, and sat on the snout. I could hear its muffled complaint, which made me sound like I was farting.

"That's not gas," I said to Linda. "I just wanted your audience to know that."

I heard all the crew members laugh out loud, and Linda did too.

"Now I see why you're a comedy star," she said.

"I believe I'm the comedy star here," Cassidy interrupted. "And I don't have to rely on costume parts and fart jokes to get a laugh. I'm the real deal."

"Let's talk about you for a minute," Linda said.

"A minute?" Cassidy said. "That's not enough time. You can barely scratch the surface of my talents. It would take the entire show just to cover my singing talent, let alone my acting ability, comedic timing, stunning good looks, innate charm, finely tuned sense of drama, and unique fashion style."

I could see Barbara Daniel standing behind the camera operators, giving Cassidy the "that's enough" sign. But Cassidy paid no attention and went on with her rant.

"Frankly, there is no end to my talent. When you've got it, you've got it." Turning to Linda, she said, "Why don't you ask me about when I first realized how talented I am? That would be a great question."

Before Linda even had a chance to ask the question, Cassidy answered it.

"I was in my crib, and I can remember standing up on my darling little legs and singing 'Twinkle, Twinkle Little Star' to all my stuffed animals. They were blown away! I crushed it."

"How did you know that?" Lisa asked. She couldn't believe what she was hearing.

"A star always knows when she's connecting with her audience. We understand the little people and the important role we play in their lives. Without us, they would have nothing. We are the inspiration for all their hopes and dreams. We are the glamour that makes their lives bearable."

Oh Cassidy, I thought. *Do you even hear yourself? What has gotten into you? Don't you know how obnoxious you sound?*

In the darkness, I could see Barbara Daniel doing something that looked like she was pulling her hair out from the roots. Chuck Smeller was dabbing sweat off his forehead with his handkerchief. This interview was not going well for them. Or for any of us.

"Why don't we talk about the special and what people can expect when they tune in this Friday?" Linda said, trying desperately to get control of the conversation. "Buddy, tell us a little bit about it."

"Well," I began, and that's all I got to say. Cassidy took over the answer.

"Basically, you'll see me being me, and by that I mean singing, dancing, acting, and being unbelievably appealing."

Linda actually held up her hand to try to stop Cassidy from talking. "Why don't we give Buddy a chance to answer?"

"Why would we do that?" Cassidy said. "Buddy's got a cute costume, but let's face it, I've got the charm. I'm the main attraction."

"Well, you certainly have more confidence than anyone I've ever interviewed," Linda said. "And that includes several presidents of the United States."

"Those people can be so boring, not like me," Cassidy

said. "All they do is run a country. I could do that with my left hand tied behind my back and still have plenty of talent left over to do my own talk show. As a matter of fact, Linda, isn't it about time for you to retire? I think I know a certain young actress right in front of you who could do a much better job."

I couldn't help myself. My six eyes spun on their track so fast that I almost fainted on the couch. What Cassidy was doing was not only damaging our special, but maybe even ruining her entire career. She was destroying everything that our fans loved about her, right there on live TV.

I made one last heroic effort to try to stop her. I jumped up on the couch, threw my arms in the air, and shouted into the camera. "Ladies and gentlemen, what you have just seen are the acting talents of Miss Cassidy Cambridge, portraying a person who has been possessed by an alien being who has overtaken her charming personality and turned her into a selfish, self-absorbed actor. If you tune in to our special, you'll see how she defeats the alien spirit and becomes herself again."

I was so into my performance that even my sensory enhancer stood straight up on my back and started to trumpet. I have to confess, it was quite a moment, until Cassidy jumped to her feet and ran right up to the camera lens.

"Don't listen to him, folks," she said, holding the sides of the camera and hogging the whole screen with her face. "What you're seeing is the real Cassidy Cambridge. The one I've kept hidden, the one who is ready to take over Hollywood, the country, the planet, and the galaxy. Get used to it, and never forget it, because I am here to stay."

"And now, let's go to a commercial break," Linda said. "When we come back, we'll show you how to make a low-calorie, gluten-free cookie that actually tastes great."

The red lights on the cameras stopped blinking, and Linda slumped down in her chair. I did too. Barbara Daniel held her head like she was trying to keep it from blowing off. Chuck Smeller had run out of forehead sweat to dab and had moved on to his armpits.

Only Cassidy looked cheerful.

"What's everyone so upset about?" she said. "I think it went great."

And that was the beginning of the end.

13

After the show, Linda Chen disappeared backstage, and Mel led Cassidy and me to the door.

"Well, you guys certainly made an impression," he said, holding the door open.

"Thank you," Cassidy answered, even though I could tell Mel certainly didn't mean it as a compliment.

Chuck Smeller and Barbara Daniel drove us back to Stage 42 without saying a word. Cassidy seemed unaware of their mood, but I could tell Ms. Daniel was steaming mad. She was rubbing her forehead and frantically reading emails and texts on her phone. Every now and then she sighed heavily. My super-duper hearing could even pick up the sound of her back teeth grinding, like she was chewing on gravel.

When we pulled up in front of our stage, Cassidy hopped

out of the golf cart with a bounce in her step, like nothing had happened.

"Cassidy, we have to talk more about this," Ms. Daniel said. "We can't just ignore the way you behaved on that show. You put the success of the special in serious jeopardy."

"I think I created a memorable television moment," Cassidy said. "People will love it, because they love me."

"That's not what social media is saying," Ms. Daniel said. "I don't even want to tell you what your so-called fans are writing. But the words *brat, spoiled, obnoxious, conceited,* and *who-does-she-think-she-is* are coming up a lot."

"That's their problem, not mine," Cassidy said. "You coming, Buddy?"

"In a minute," I answered. "I'll be right in."

I waited behind so I could have a word with Ms. Daniel.

"Cassidy will get over this," I said after Cassidy was out of view. "It's just a phase. She's been talking to Mr. Hitchcock, and he's filled her head with a lot of big ideas."

"And who is this Mr. Hitchcock, other than someone who is ruining our show?"

"He's a very important film director who's about to cast Cassidy and Tyler in his next movie."

"If he's so important, why haven't I heard of him?" Ms. Daniel wondered. "There are all kinds of people in

Hollywood who think they're star makers. Most of them are full of baloney."

"I had baloney once," I said. "With mustard. My two tongues loved it."

"Buddy, you can knock off the alien routine now. I'm busy. Chuck, get me what's-her-name on the phone."

"What's-her-name who?" Mr. Smeller asked.

"You know. The network crisis manager, the one who fixed that problem with the star of our Vampire series."

"Oh, I remember that," Mr. Smeller said. "The actor who actually bit his costar on the neck with his false fang. The press had a field day with that."

"Until what's-her-name convinced them to write about something else," Ms. Daniel said. "What is her name again? Sheri something or other . . ."

Chuck had already pulled out both his phones and was scrolling through his contacts.

"I have Sheri Diamond, Sheri Grimes, Sheri Stroganoff, Sheri Woodley, Sheri Cherry, Sheri Clutterbuck, Sheri Ramos, Sheri Mender . . ."

"That's it!" Ms. Daniel said. "She's the one. Sheri Mender. Call her and tell her to meet me in my office right away. I'll get her to straighten Cassidy out."

"Oh, I'm sure Cassidy would like to be straightened

out," I said, trying to be positive. "Posture is very important to her."

"Just go inside now, Buddy," Ms. Daniel said. "That's cute but we have serious things to take care of, and I don't have time for cute."

Even though I was being totally serious, I made a mental note never to be cute around network executives. Apparently, it's a no-no. I still have so much to learn about humans in Hollywood.

As soon as I walked into the sound stage, I heard a commotion coming from the cafeteria set. Everyone was gathered around Cassidy, talking all at once. Obviously, they had seen *Star Roundup* because the whole cast was furious.

"I don't know what you were trying to accomplish," Martha said to her, "but it looked like you were trying out for Jerk of the Year."

"Or like Darth Vader had overtaken your brain," Ulysses added. Then dropping his voice to a low growl, he did a perfect imitation of Darth himself. "I am Cassidy, and I have gone to the dark side. Evil lives within me, so beware."

"I *told* them they should have asked me to be on the show," Tyler said. "But did they listen? No. Instead they chose you, and now look at the mess we're in."

"Hey man, go easy on Cassidy," Luis said, always ready

to defend her. "She's just having a little case of nerves. When some people get stressed, they get diarrhea, and other people get diarrhea of the mouth. Right, Cassidy?"

"Eeuuww. That is the grossest thing anyone has ever said to me."

"Just trying to help," Luis said.

"Well, stop trying," she snapped back. "In fact, all of you leave me alone."

"Cassidy, try to understand," Duane said. "We were counting on you to promote our special, but you didn't. Instead, you promoted yourself, and in a very rude and offensive way. Why would anyone tune in to see our show now?"

"You call it rude and offensive, but I call it star power," Cassidy said. "Everybody's already talking about me."

"But not in a good way," Duane said. "You were supposed to be representing all of us, and let's face it, you let us down big time. This is terrible publicity for the show."

"Mr. Hitchcock says there's no such thing as bad publicity," Cassidy said. "He says all attention is good as long as they spell your name right. And mine is C-A-S-S-I-D-Y."

Duane just shook his head.

"I've seen this happen to other child stars and it's really sad," he said. "Success goes to their heads, they become obsessed with their own fame, then they crash and burn. For your sake and for ours, I hope you can pull yourself out of this."

"Oh, she will, Duane," I said. "I'm sure of it. I know Cassidy. We all do. Inside she's sweet and kind and full of love. Aren't you, Cass?"

I winked at her with eyes number two and three. Ever since I came to Earth, I'd been working on perfecting my wink. It's not an easy thing to learn when you have six eyes, but I had finally gotten the hang of it. This was the first time I had used my wink in public. I thought it was charming, but apparently Cassidy didn't.

"Your eyeballs are twitching, dude," she said. "You should put some drops in them."

Duane picked up his script and moved to the center of the cafeteria set.

"All right, folks," he said. "Might as well make the best show we can, so let's get to work. It's already Wednesday and we have a special to tape on Friday. Who can tell me how many days that gives us?"

"Two!" Martha belted out, her soprano voice trilling like a sparrow in spring.

"Wow, Martha, I didn't know you could sing and subtract at the same time," Tyler said. "You're a double threat."

"I prefer to think of myself as a double scoop of chocolate chip ice cream, hold the whipped cream."

We got down to work. Duane had us rehearse the last scene of the show, the one where the aliens board their spaceship to return home. He brought Stan, our head writer, out on set to help us decide which cast member would go with the aliens. Tyler wanted it to be him, because as he walked up the spaceship ramp, he could assume a body-building pose that showed off his pecs. Martha wanted it to be her so she could sing a sad farewell ballad with a moody blue spotlight. Ulysses thought it should be him since he already had an excellent Darth Vader impression.

"I think we can end this discussion now," Cassidy said, rising from the canvas chair where she had draped herself. "There is only one person who should command the star moment, and I think we all know who that is."

"Logically it should be Buddy, since he's playing an alien," Stan said.

"That just shows your lack of imagination," Cassidy said. "Show business demands big personalities, not tiny thinkers."

Stan took his pencil from behind his ear, threw it on the floor, and stomped off.

"Maybe you have to listen to this, but I don't," he said to Duane as he left.

"Let's take five." Duane let out an exasperated sigh. "Cassidy, I need to speak with you right away."

Duane never got to have his talk with her, because just as he pulled her aside, the stage door flew open and Barbara Daniel came strutting in, with Chuck Smeller following behind. Ms. Daniel was accompanied by another woman in a dark gray suit, whose face looked like it had a permanent frown carved into it. She was clearly not a person who was on this Earth to have a good time.

"Sorry to interrupt again," Ms. Daniel said to Duane, "but we need to talk to Cassidy immediately."

"Good, maybe you can talk some sense into her," Duane said.

"Buddy, I want you to come too," Ms. Daniel said. "Where can we talk in private?"

"The classroom would be good," I suggested. "No one's in school now, and our teacher, Janice, went home for the day."

"Follow me, both of you," the woman with the frown said.

"Who died and left you boss?" Cassidy said.

Without answering, the woman spun on her heels and marched to the classroom at the back of our set. I marched right behind her, while Cassidy shuffled reluctantly behind.

"Take a seat, kids," Ms. Daniel said, pointing to the classroom table and chairs. "This is Sheri Mender. She's employed by the network to help us fix major problems that arise. We call it crisis management."

"Good," said Cassidy, "because I have a major problem myself. I'm thirsty and I need a lemonade with extra ice."

"I'm not here to bring you cold drinks," Ms. Mender said.

"Then exactly why *are* you here?"

"Because you appeared on an important talk show today and let your mouth run like a broken faucet. What you said was unpleasant, impolite, and destructive. The internet is flooded with negative comments about you that could ruin the success of the show."

"What you call unpleasant, I call entertaining," Cassidy

said. "My conversation was gripping. I could feel that I had the audience in the palm of my hand."

"Allow me to point out that there was no audience," Ms. Mender said, "so whatever you had in the palm of your hand was only in your imagination."

"Maybe it was that cucumber-scented hand lotion you use," I suggested.

"Buddy, enough," Ms. Daniel said. "Cassidy, we need you to release an official apology to the press. Ms. Mender has prepared one. Chuck, do you have it with you?"

"You bet, boss." Mr. Smeller reached into his pocket and pulled out a sheet of white paper. He laid it down on the table and handed Cassidy a pen. "Just sign on the dotted line and we'll release it to all the media."

"What does it say?"

"Simply that you were suffering from extreme stress due to the pressures of the show, and your nerves got the better of you. You said things you didn't mean and you're very, very sorry."

"That sounds great, Cass," I said. "I think that's what actually happened because stress is very stressful, and when you're stressed, you say things you wouldn't say if you weren't stressed."

Cassidy glared at me.

"First of all, what you just said makes no sense. And second of all, I am not stressed. I'm happy. I'm successful. I'm me."

"Sounds like the title of some phony self-help book," Ms. Mender said.

"It's a direct quote from Mr. Hitchcock."

"Well, whoever he is, he needs a rewrite. Now if you'll just sign the apology statement, we can get this off to everyone who matters."

"I'm not signing it," Cassidy said. "And that's final."

Ms. Daniel pulled up one of the classroom chairs next to Cassidy and spoke to her in a comforting voice. "Cassidy, dear, I anticipated something like this, so I took the liberty of calling your mother. I know how much you value her opinion and I thought she could talk to you."

"Sorry, my mother's at Space Camp."

"Yes, I know. I called her there and they had to pull her out of arts and crafts. Apparently, they were making solar systems from Styrofoam balls. She was very grateful."

"That's a big project if you include all the moons of Jupiter," I said. "There are seventy-nine of them, and we're discovering new ones every year."

I thought that fact was fascinating, but apparently, no one else did.

"Save the astronomy lesson," Ms. Mender snapped. "Go on, Barbara."

"So when your mother heard about the show, she was very upset. She agreed to leave immediately."

"What about my whiny little sister?"

"The camp put her in charge of handing out s'mores, so she's fine. For every one she hands out, she eats two. Anyway, your mother is on her way back to the studio to advise you."

"How? She didn't even take her car. She went on the camp bus with Eloise."

"I tried to order her a car, but there was no limo service in the area," Chuck Smeller said. Then he added proudly, "But I was able to talk a camp counselor into giving her a ride on the camp motorcycle."

Cassidy laughed for the first time that day.

"My mother riding on the back of a motorcycle? No way that's happening."

"Actually, she isn't riding *on* the motorcycle," Mr. Smeller said, trying to stifle a little chuckle. "She's riding *in* the motorcycle. It apparently has a side car, which the camp uses to transport its garbage to the composting dump."

"Oh, this gets better every second," Cassidy said. "I can see it now."

"Apparently she wasn't happy about the garbage, but they

managed to find a plastic tarp for her to sit on," Ms. Daniel explained. "Chuck, can you check to see if we've heard from her?"

Mr. Smeller picked up both phones and checked the screens. It really was quite impressive how he could operate one phone with each hand.

"This one says they're at the studio gate now," he said. "And this one says they're here. They made very good time for a garbage motorcycle."

"That makes sense," I commented. "After all, the garbage bin was empty, so it had no weight. Therefore, it would be able go at top speed. Everyone knows that the speed of an object is inversely proportional to the mass."

"What are you, some kind of walking science book?" Ms. Mender asked.

"I'm not just your average good-looking alien," I said modestly.

We heard the clomping of Delores's space boots before she even entered the classroom. When the door flew open, both Cassidy and I gasped at the sight of her. Her hair was blown in a thousand different directions and her red lipstick had spread all the way up her cheeks. As she passed by me, I detected the faint odor of old baloney and older swiss cheese. Then I saw the source of the aroma. Delores had a half-eaten baloney sandwich stuck to her butt. I knew she wouldn't want to be seen in such an embarrassing position, so I decided to speak up.

"Excuse me, Delores," I began, "but you seem to have some luncheon meat scraps attached to your ... uh ... rear quarters."

She was too preoccupied to respond. She reached around and yanked the sandwich remains off her skirt and tossed them toward the wastebasket, missing by a mile. Then she turned to Cassidy and got right up in her face.

"Look at this position you put me in, Cassidy," she yelled. "Do you know I had to ride in a moving garbage bin to get here? What were you thinking? Didn't I tell you to be sweet and charming? Haven't I trained you to always be professional? Did your mouth forget what your brain was telling it to do?"

"That's five questions, Mom," Cassidy answered, pulling her phone from her jeans pocket and switching on a game. "You've reached your limit."

Ms. Mender took Delores by the arm and spoke to her in a confidential voice. "We need you to get Cassidy to sign a public apology. It is of utmost importance. We have the paper right here."

"She'll sign it right now. Won't you, Cassidy?"

"No."

"Then suppose you tell me what the problem is."

Cassidy looked up from her screen. "The problem is I asked for lemonade and no one has gotten me any," she said.

The two executives and Mr. Smeller let out a gasp in unison. It was such a disrespectful thing to say that even Delores was embarrassed, and she didn't embarrass easily. She tried to cover for Cassidy by turning on her most charming smile.

"Cassidy is simply impossible when she's thirsty," Delores said in the most fake cheerful voice I'd ever heard. "She's been like that ever since she was a toddler, haven't you, honey?"

"If you say so, Mom."

"Mrs. Cambridge," Barbara Daniel said. "I have to tell you that we've already heard from our sponsor, who is threatening to remove all their advertising from *Oddball Academy*. That means we might have to cancel the show."

Now it was time for Delores to gasp.

"That would be a disaster," she said.

"Double disaster plus a catastrophe." Ms. Mender nodded. "They are saying they don't want to be in business with Cassidy. No one wants their chicken noodle soup associated with a snotty star."

"Shoot, my avatar just died," Cassidy said.

Delores snatched the phone from Cassidy and tossed it across the room. It landed on the navy-blue bean bag chair we sit in when we're studying for tests.

"Mom! I was playing that game."

"Not anymore you're not. Did you hear that you're going to lose your sponsors if you don't shape up?"

"So we'll get another sponsor. Nobody likes their chicken noodle soup anyway. It's so salty and the chicken chunks aren't even real."

"Delores," Barbara Daniel said. "We need that sponsor. They pay for the show. And they are threatening to jump ship today."

"Okay, okay," Delores said, pacing the room. "Can I talk to them now? I'll reassure them that Cassidy will get back on track. Then I'll deal with her."

"We should go to my office and try to get on a conference call with them," Ms. Daniel said. "Quick action is necessary."

"But Cassidy stays here," Ms. Mender said. "Until she can keep her lips zipped."

Delores leaned down and whispered in my ear. "I'll go with them. You talk to Cassidy. I need your help. I'm counting on you."

The adults hurried out of the classroom, and suddenly it was very quiet. I took a deep breath and looked at Cassidy.

She looked the same as always on the outside, but inside, she was a different person.

"What are you staring at?" she asked.

"I want to talk to you."

"Well, I don't want to talk to you. I want to call Mr. Hitchcock, I have such a special connection with him, and he's the only one who believes in me."

"That's not true. We all believe in you."

"It's not the same. When I hear his words, it's like he's inside my brain, making me feel strong and powerful."

"His words are making you into someone you're not," I said. "He's taking away all your good qualities—the kindness, the joy, the heart filled with love. All the things that make you human."

"What would you know about being human? You're an alien."

"I've been learning how to be a human from you. And you know what? I like what I've become. You humans are good people, and you have been a great role model."

"Mr. Hitchcock is making me a real movie star," she said. "It's what I've always wanted. And you should be grateful for that, because I can take you along with me. He's told me he thinks you have star power too."

"Well, I don't want to be a star if it means being mean and rude and self-important."

"Are you saying that's what I am?"

"I'm saying that since you've met Mr. Hitchcock, that's how you've been acting."

There was a knock on the door, and Duane stuck his head in.

"Cassidy, if you want to be the one who boards the alien ship, we're blocking the scene. Buddy, I'll need you in a few minutes."

"You go," I said to Cassidy. "We can finish this conversation later."

"I'm done with this conversation," she said, getting up to leave. "See ya, don't wanna be ya."

She followed Duane out the door. As they left, I could hear her telling him to have the production assistant bring her a lemonade and an oatmeal cookie, no raisins.

I just sat there for a minute, trying to think of any way I could talk some sense into her. As I stared blankly around the room, my eyes fell on her phone still sitting on the navy-blue bean bag chair. I walked over to get it, and even though I knew I shouldn't, I clicked on her recent phone calls. The screen flashed and the last phone number she had called came up. It was Howard Hitchcock's.

I didn't recognize the area code. In my mind, I ran through all the hundreds of thousands of area codes that were programmed into my brain, but his didn't come up. He must be even more important than I had thought, to have his own secret area code.

Once again, I knew I shouldn't, but I dialed the number.

"Greetings," came the answer.

"Mr. Hitchcock, it's Buddy Burger."

"I know."

"I need to talk to you right away."

"I know."

"It's about Cassidy."

"I know."

"How do you know?

"Let's just say, I know everything about you."

"That's impossible."

"Come see me and I'll prove it to you," he said. "Meet me on the back lot. I'll be waiting at the entrance to the

mechanical shark show. I like sharks. Did you know they have no eyelids? And that they can hear their prey's heartbeat just before they kill them? I find that amusing."

He laughed and I felt a chill tiptoe down my spine.

Despite my own fast-beating heart, I knew what I had to do.

"I'll be right there," I said and hung up the phone.

14

Just as he promised, **Mr. Hitchcock was waiting for** me at the entrance to the mechanical shark attraction. Zelda was dozing on his shoulder, her beak snuggly tucked into her chest. The shark attraction is based on a famous movie called *Jaws*, where a gigantic great white shark terrifies a whole oceanside town. As part of the studio tour, the trams travel along the side of a lake and then the mechanical shark used in the movie jumps out of the water and scares the stuffing out of the tourists.

It's an eerie place, and the presence of weird Mr. Hitchcock made it seem even creepier.

"Welcome to my shark tank," Mr. Hitchcock said as I hurried up to him.

He held out his gloved hand to shake mine and when I took hold of it, I felt what seemed like a current of electricity. This must have been what Cassidy felt when she shook

hands with him on the set. I wondered if maybe he was raised next to a power grid. Instinctively, I pulled my hand away.

"That's quite a grip you've got there," I said.

"A leader needs a strong grip to control his subjects."

"Subjects? I thought you were a director."

"Of course I am. I think of my cast and crew as my subjects."

"Wow, how do they feel about that?"

"I've never asked them. They have no choice in the matter."

I heard someone calling my name and turned around to see one of the tourist trams approaching the entrance to the shark exhibit. I had been spotted.

"Hey, look, there's the alien from *Oddball Academy*," someone called.

"Love your work," a little kid shouted.

And before I knew it, everyone on the tram had their cell phones out and were snapping pictures of me.

"Buddy, come over here and pose with my daughter," a man called. "It's her tenth birthday."

"Will you excuse me a minute," I asked Mr. Hitchcock. "I need to go take that picture. After all, it's the kid's tenth birthday."

"I will not excuse you, and I don't care if it's her four hundredth birthday. We have business to conduct, and I don't have time for this foolishness. I'll find a place with fewer distractions. Follow me."

Mr. Hitchcock pushed open the gate that said DO NOT ENTER and headed toward a shed that said EMPLOYEES ONLY. When I hesitated, he turned around and said, "What are you waiting for? I commanded you to follow me."

"Look at the sign," I said. "It says we're not supposed to enter."

"That's for everyday people. I make my own rules. Now come with me."

I followed him to the shed, where he tried to open the door, but it was locked. He poked Zelda, who woke up with a startled squawk.

"Pick open the lock," he ordered her. "That ugly beak has to be good for something."

Zelda flew off his shoulder and perched herself on the doorknob of the shed. Leaning down, she attacked the padlock like a vulture, pecking and squawking and clawing at it until the poor lock just gave up and fell on the ground. Mr. Hitchcock pushed the door open and entered a room filled with churning machinery. It was obviously the control room for the shark attraction. No one was there. The only sign of human life was a lunch box that was labeled MANNY SORENTO, sitting on a wooden worktable.

"We can talk here," Mr. Hitchcock said. "We have ten minutes until this fool Manny Sorento, whoever he is, comes back from his break."

"How do you know how long his break is?" I asked.

"They take them every hour. These people don't know the meaning of work. In my world, there's no such thing as a break."

"You don't give your cast and crew time to rest?" I thought of Duane, who gave us breaks to get snacks whenever our energy seemed to lag. This guy was like a dictator who didn't care about his people. I was nervous to bring up the subject of Cassidy, but there was no time like the present to dive in.

"Sir, I need to talk to you about Cassidy," I began.

"I already know what you're going to say," he answered. "You don't like the way she's behaving. You don't like her attitude. You don't recognize her anymore. She's changed in a way you don't understand and don't like."

"That's exactly what I was going to say," I said. "Are you a mind reader?"

"My mind has powers beyond your comprehension. With the right subjects, I am able to control their thoughts."

"I don't believe you," I said. "Show me."

"Give me your hand," he said, reaching out to take mine in his. He held it as if we were shaking hands. "Concentrate carefully on my voice. You will feel your brain start to hear my words inside your head, as if they are your own thoughts."

As I listened to his voice, I began to realize that the thoughts I was having were not my own. It was happening just like he said. I heard his voice in my head instructing me to go to the lunchbox, open it, and take a bite of the tuna sandwich inside. I hate tuna fish, but nevertheless, I let go of his hand, walked to the lunchbox, opened it, and took out the plastic baggie that contained two tuna sandwiches. I took one out, but just before I took a bite, static replaced his voice in my head, and I could no longer understand the commands he was giving me. I put the sandwich back in the bag and slammed the lunchbox shut.

He seemed surprised.

"I thought I told you to take a bite of that sandwich," he said.

"That sandwich isn't mine. Someone else is looking forward to eating it. And I don't want it."

"You have a strong mind and a stronger will," Mr. Hitchcock said. "It's clear that my powers are not working on you. You're not as suggestible as your friend Cassidy is."

"Is that what you've done to her? Control her thoughts?"

"She's not entirely sure of who she is, so she has an open pathway. It makes my job much easier."

"Her mother is always making her doubt herself, always telling her what to do," I said. "You saw her weakness and you're preying on her."

Mr. Hitchcock laughed. "Yes, like a shark destroys its prey."

"Why are you doing this to her? She's such a good person and so talented with a big future in front of her. You're taking it all away. If she continues along the path you've set her on, her life will be ruined and her dreams will be squashed."

"I know," he said. He sounded very pleased with himself.

"Then give her back her personality. The one that we know and love."

"I am prepared to do just that," Mr. Hitchcock said.

A wave of relief swept over me. I had gotten to this man and convinced him to do the right thing.

"Thank you," I said, turning to leave. "You won't be sorry."

"Not so fast, Mr. Buddy Burger. Or should I say Citizen Short Nose."

I froze in my tracks.

"How could you possibly know that name?"

"I told you I know all things, especially about *you*."

I felt my heart beat faster and faster like it was going to explode out of my chest. My forehead broke into a cold sweat.

"Who . . . are . . . you . . . ?" My voice shook. I feared I knew the answer to my own question.

"Let me introduce myself," he said.

In one swift and violent gesture, he reached up to the top of his head and ripped off his pith helmet along with the mosquito net covering his face. There he was, in all his ugliness.

The Supreme Leader.

He was even more grotesque than I had remembered. The Earth's atmosphere had dried his face so much that his skin was flaking off like fish scales. His cobalt-blue color had faded to a sickly gray, and his red gums were twisted into a demented, crazy smile.

I gasped when I saw him, my three lungs struggling to take in enough air so I wouldn't pass out.

"Happy to see me?" he asked. "I bring you greetings from your home."

I tried to talk, but no words came out. Only another rasping breath that sounded like the wind howling through an abandoned house.

"When Citizen Cruel failed in her mission to return you to us, I took it upon myself to pay you a little visit. She was very helpful in leading me right to you."

"That's impossible. Citizen Cruel is locked up in a concrete box in a secret government facility."

"Oh really?" Then turning to Zelda, he gave the parrot a hard poke that brought her to attention. "Did you hear where he thinks you are?"

"*Squawk!*" Zelda shrieked. "He's stupid! Always was! *Squawk!*"

"You underestimate my powers, Citizen Short Nose," the Supreme Leader said. "You're just like your grandmother.

You think you can defy me. Your family will never learn the extent of my powers. I have come to take you home and teach you a lesson."

I stared at the parrot and saw the familiar golden glow coming from her eyes. It was the same light that Citizen Cruel emitted in all her attempts to kidnap me. I knew she was a shape-shifter, but I never dreamed she could turn into a talking, squawking parrot. I backed away from her, remembering how merciless she had been in pursuit of me. Whether she was a parrot or an alien, she was cruel through and through, but this time I wasn't going to let her see my fear.

"You failed," I said to Zelda—actually to Citizen Cruel, who was living inside of her. "You could not capture me, and neither will he."

"Oh, that's where you're sadly mistaken," the Supreme Leader said, his lips turning into a vicious grin. "I have a secret weapon, and her name is Cassidy Cambridge."

"You leave her out of this!" I could hear myself shouting.

"I'm afraid that's impossible now," he said, his voice so calm and cold that it made my purple blood freeze in my veins. "As you've seen, I have control of Cassidy's mind. And whether or not I return her to herself is up to you."

"Tell me what I have to do, and I'll do it."

"It's very simple, my short-nosed friend. Return with me to our planet, and I will return Cassidy to her former self. All will be as it should be."

"You wouldn't do that to me!"

"Oh yes he would!" Zelda squawked.

"You're making me chose between Cassidy's future and my own. That's an impossible choice."

Zelda squawked and cackled at the same time. It was an ugly sound.

"You have no choice, loser! *Squawk!*"

The Supreme Leader stroked Zelda on her feathered head. "That's a good bird," he said. "When we return to our planet, maybe I will reinstate you into the Squadron."

"Thank you, Supreme Leader!" she cackled contentedly. "I will serve you forever! *Squawk!*"

There was no sound in the shed except for the churning of the machines and the cackling of the cruel parrot. My mind was going a mile a minute, trying to come up with a way out of this horrible dilemma.

"What's it going to be, Short Nose?" the Supreme Leader said. "Surrender yourself to me and I will free the girl's mind. Refuse and I'll ruin her."

I felt caught, trapped like a fly in a spider's web. Then I

heard footsteps crunching on the gravel outside the shed, followed by the squeaking of the doorknob. The door burst open and a man with a large mustache stared at us.

"Hey," he said. "Didn't you read the sign? No entrance. Employees only. This is my work shed."

"We're so sorry, sir," I said, "but I'm very glad to see you. You must be Manny."

"That's me, and I know you. You're the guy who plays the alien on that TV show my kids watch. I like your work. And who are you supposed to be," he said, turning to the Supreme Leader. "Grandpa Alien? The oldest guy on the kid's planet?"

"Who are you supposed to be?" the Supreme Leader shot back. "The man with the hairiest upper lip on this planet? How do you eat those two sandwiches of yours without chomping on all that hair?"

"Hey, what are you doing sniffing around in my lunchbox?" Manny said. "That's technically your second break-in. The first was my shed. I don't like your attitude."

"I don't like anything about you," the Supreme Leader said. "You're just another lowly rat who works here."

"Okay, that's it. I've heard enough," Manny said. "I'm

calling security. I was willing to overlook your break-ins because you're on TV and all, but this is too much."

Manny picked up an old-fashioned land line phone from the wooden table and punched in a number.

"Security, I got a problem here at the *Jaws* machinery shed. I need you over here as soon as possible."

The Supreme Leader lunged for the phone, but I could tell his body was weak, and his lunge fell short as he tripped over the telephone wire. Zelda took off from his shoulder and flew in Manny's face, flapping her wings above his head to block his view. I took the opportunity to bolt, charging out the door and down the gravel path. I ran on my tiptoes so my suction cups wouldn't slow me down. I didn't stop until I reached Stage 42.

Cassidy was inside there, and I needed to warn her that her fate was in the hands of a cruel and heartless being.

I hoped I could get through to her. Her entire future depended on it.

15

When I burst onto the stage, Stan and Duane were at the table in deep discussion. Delores, still in her space boots, was pacing back and forth. Cassidy was slouched in her chair, painting her nails a lime green. The whole place smelled like nail polish, but she didn't seem to care. She wasn't paying any attention to the heated conversation that was going on at the table, either.

I ran right up to her and said, "I need to talk to you. It's urgent."

"Buddy," said Delores. "Your timing has always been terrible. What we are discussing couldn't be more urgent. The network is demanding that we cut Cassidy from the special."

"But she's the heart of the show," I protested.

"Used to be," Duane said. "Apparently, her fans are bailing on her by the thousands. The sponsors are going to pull out if she stays."

"No sponsors, no show," Stan said. "No show, no script. No script, no writer. And poof, I'm out of a job. We're all out of a job."

"Maybe you can find another job you're better at," Cassidy snarled, "because you're sure not great at writing."

"Cassidy!" Delores said. "Watch your mouth. You're going to lose everything if you don't cut this out right away."

"Speaking of which," Duane said, "Barbara Daniel informed me that the shoe company who created your personal sneakers is firing you as spokesperson."

"No!" Delores moaned. "Not the sneakers."

"They were ugly anyway," Cassidy said. "The color made my feet barf."

"You see," Duane said, shaking his finger at Cassidy. "No one wants to be associated with you. You're toxic."

"She is not toxic," Delores said. "She's momentarily out of her mind."

"And I know the reason why," I interrupted.

They all waited for me to go on, but as soon as I said the words, I realized I couldn't reveal the truth: Mr. Hitchcock was actually the Supreme Leader. I would be forced to confess I was an alien, and if I did that, they would call the FBI and lock me up forever and then I would never be able to help Cassidy break his spell over her.

"Tell us," Duane said. "What is it, Buddy? What's going on with her?"

"I've got to talk to her by herself. It's something you would never understand."

"Listen here, you're not going to leave me out of this conversation," Delores said. "I'm her mother, and I've known everything about her since the day she was born. I know not only that she pooped blueberries into her diapers but that she pooped them whole."

That got Cassidy's attention.

"Mom, if you keep talking like that, I'll fire you as my manager."

"You can't. We have a contract."

"Mr. Hitchcock says contracts were made to be ripped up," Cassidy said, blowing on her fingernails to dry the polish.

"Oh really. Well, where was Mr. Hitchcock when you burned your mouth on a piece of pepperoni pizza and I had to soak your tongue in a glass of ice for hours on end?"

"Oh, you're going to bring that up again?" Cassidy said. "Well how about when you and dad were separating, and I had to listen to your complaints about his snoring in your ear all night."

Stan cleared his throat. "Uh . . . this is getting awfully

personal," he said. "Maybe you guys want to have some privacy to work this out."

"Let's go into my dressing room," I said.

"Luis is in there, running his lines," Duane said.

"Fine, we'll go in yours," I said to Cassidy, practically yanking her out of her chair. "There isn't a second to waste."

"Don't touch my nails," she snapped. "You'll smudge them."

"Just hurry."

Delores followed Cassidy and me into the dressing room. Cassidy flopped on the couch and pulled out her cell phone.

"Do not call Mr. Hitchcock," I said. "You're not going to believe me, but he's the problem."

"Just spit it out, Buddy," Delores said. "What are you saying?"

"Mr. Hitchcock is in possession of your brain," I said to Cassidy as bluntly as I could. "He has entered your mind and is putting false ideas into your head. All of your obnoxious thoughts and actions are controlled by him."

"He's teaching me to be my own person," Cassidy protested.

"Well, that person has just lost her job," Delores snorted. "I think it's time to show Mr. Hitchcock to the door. His time with you is up."

"Says who?" Cassidy said, slamming her phone down on the makeup table. "I make my own decisions now."

"No you don't," I said. "Mr. Hitchcock is in charge of you. And when I confronted him about that, he refused to stop unless..."

I stopped dead in my tracks and looked over at Delores. She couldn't know the "unless" part.

"Unless what?" Cassidy demanded to know. "What's he want you to do?"

"Tell us, Buddy," Delores said. "Why are you being so secretive? As your manager, I thought we shared everything."

"Well, not quite everything. The next part gets complicated."

"I'm listening," Delores said. "You have two seconds to spill it out."

I took a deep breath.

"Okay," I began. "Fasten your seat belt, because this is going to be a bumpy ride. Here goes. Mr. Hitchcock isn't really Mr. Hitchcock. He is my Supreme Leader from back home."

"In Wisconsin?"

"A little farther, actually. I'm not really from Wisconsin."

"I always suspected that," Delores said. "You don't

have that accent, and you don't eat cheese. So where are you from and why are you calling that jerky guy your supreme leader?"

"Tell her already, Buddy," Cassidy said, "so we can get out of here. My nails need a second coat and I left the nail polish on the cast table."

"Delores, I am actually an alien," I said. "Not a pretend alien. Not a character on a television show, but a real one."

She didn't react, so I went on.

"I come from a red dwarf planet thousands of light-years away. I fled my planet in a spaceship my grandmother built to escape the evil government of the Supreme Leader. Mr. Hitchcock is the Supreme Leader in disguise. He's come to Earth to kidnap me and take me home. He has taken over Cassidy's mind and made her behave in a way that will ruin her career in order to get to me. He will not release her until I agree to go with him."

There, it was out in the open, just hanging in the air.

Delores thought intently while I waited for her reaction. I could see the wheels in her brain turning. The silence in the room was deafening. Even Cassidy remained quiet while we waited and waited and waited. At last, Delores spoke.

"Okay, Buddy, you've had your fun now. So let's quit the

nonsense and tell me the truth, because while you're horsing around with this goofball story, the writers are outside cutting Cassidy's role down to nothing."

"It *is* the truth, Delores."

I turned to Cassidy, who was watching with curiosity. "Your mind isn't your own," I said to her. "The Supreme Leader has you in his spell, and he's evil. This guy doesn't stop until he gets what he wants. That's how he took over my whole planet, changing it from a happy society into a joyless, miserable existence for all the citizens."

"Buddy, if you keep this nonsense up, it's going to ruin your career too," Delores said. "Both of you have lost your minds. Maybe there's something in the water at the studio. I'm going to call Dr. Posner."

She reached into her purse and fished around for her phone, which was never far from her ear.

"Don't bother, Delores," I said.

"There's nothing Dr. Posner can do," Cassidy added, "unless he's got a medical book on treating aliens. Did you know Buddy has two tongues and three lungs? Hey, that rhymes. Maybe I should be a poet if they fire me. I'll be a star poet. I'll have my own line of sneakers with poems all over them."

"All right. That's it. I've had enough," Delores said,

opening the dressing room door. "If you're not going to get serious and cooperate, I'm going to go ahead and tell them to write you out of the show. Both of you."

"Wait, Delores. I'll prove to you that we're telling the truth," I said. "Close the door. Sit down."

She closed the door but did not sit down. Instead, she leaned on the makeup table and started drumming the top of it with her fingernails. Her nails sounded like a rat's claws running across a tile floor. The sound was distracting as I took hold of my amulet and tried to concentrate.

"*Be Zane*," I murmured. "*Be Zane now.*"

Nothing happened. I couldn't concentrate. The tap-tap-tapping of Delores's fingernails on the table was distracting me. I dug down deep into my powers of concentration and continued to chant. Then I felt them, the human hairs on my head starting to sprout from my bald alien bumps. They appeared in clusters until I had a full head of hair. Then I felt my human skin descending down my face to cover my six eyes until I was left with only two brown human eyes. They could see Delores, her mouth hanging open and her eyes as wide as dinner plates.

I knew she was terrified. What human wouldn't be to see an alien transformation in progress? But I knew I had to keep going so she could see the real me, the whole me.

Clutching the amulet tightly, I continued to chant until I could feel the human skin covering my red gums and replacing them with lips and teeth. I smiled at Delores, thinking that might calm her down, but apparently it had the opposite effect. She screamed like she had seen a zombie.

"Arrrggghhhhh! Gaaaaasssppp! Yiiiiikkkkes!"

There aren't enough scream sounds on your planet to even describe the sounds that came pouring out of her throat.

My biological alteration came to an abrupt halt. There was no way I could concentrate on finishing it with all the ruckus and noise pollution that was taking place inside the dressing room. There I was, with a full-blown human face attached to the body of an alien.

"Eeuuw, you look gross!" Cassidy said. "That half-and-half thing is creepy. Like that time you had one alien leg stuck on your human body."

"You . . . you . . . you've seen him do this before?" Delores stammered.

"Tons of times."

"Then there really is an alien in my house? Sleeping down the hall from me? In my kitchen? Eating my avocados?"

"And soaking in your bathtub," I added.

She started to scream again. I had to do something to calm her down.

"Would you like to see how my sensory enhancer works?" I asked. "It's really kind of fun. It responds to smells and tastes in a very entertaining way."

I reached over to the makeup table and picked up a bottle of scented room spray. I gave it a squirt and a lemony smell filled the air. When my sensory enhancer got a whiff of that, it sprang into action. Swirling in big circles, it sniffed and snorted with deep inhaled breaths. Once activated, it went on the hunt for other smells, making wild pig noises as it searched for more stimulation. Then it caught a smell coming from Delores's purse and flung itself inside, rifling around until it emerged with a cinnamon-scented breath mint. My sensory inhancer inhaled so hard that you could almost feel the air leaving the room.

"It really likes cinnamon," Cassidy commented. "Look, it's starting to drool."

That was too much for Delores. Her eyes rolled so far back in her head that I could see only the whites of her eyeballs. The last thing I heard was a gurgling sound coming from her throat before she flopped headfirst onto the makeup table, her nose landing in a jar of gooey face cleanser. False eyelashes stuck to her lips like hairy caterpillars. Various shades of green eyeshadow splotched her face, making her skin look like pond scum.

Poor Delores. It was not a glamorous look.

"Are you going to help?" I asked Cassidy. "In case you didn't notice, your mom just fainted."

"She'll come around eventually," Cassidy said with a

shrug. Wow, the Supreme Leader really had a vice grip on her personality. She was as cold as ice.

I tried to revive Delores by shaking her shoulders gently. For a moment, her eyes fluttered open. But when she saw that my hand with its seven spiny fingers and three-inch-long fingernails was touching her shoulder, she screamed and passed out again, this time for real.

She was out cold.

16

We loaded Delores into a golf cart and took her to the small studio hospital that was just beyond the *Jurassic World* water ride. Luis drove and we used Cassidy's bathrobe belt to strap a muttering Delores into the passenger seat next to him.

I had turned myself back into my full alien body. I thought that would attract less attention than my half-boy, half-alien look. When we dragged Delores across the sound stage, we told Duane that she had fainted from eating the horrible camp food. He was just glad to see that I was in costume so I'd be ready for rehearsal. He gave me thirty minutes to accompany Delores to the infirmary, but told me I had to be back on set promptly to go over the new scenes.

"What about me?" Cassidy asked him.

"You can stay with your mother for as long as you like," Duane said. "You're out of the script."

"Fine," Cassidy answered in a snippy tone. "I have other plans for my career. This show was never worth my time anyway. Mr. Hitchcock said it was just a stepping-stone."

Even though I had told her that Mr. Hitchcock was the Supreme Leader, the information had not sunk in. That's how strong his influence was on her mind.

As we drove from our sound stage to the back lot, Delores was barely able to hold her head up. It wobbled on her neck like one of those bobblehead figures they have in the tourist souvenir shops at the studio. I have never understood why you humans find it so amusing to own a doll whose head is constantly about to drop off. But then I've never understood basketball either. Why would a bunch of grown people run from one end of a long room to the other, bouncing a rather large ball?

Delores was babbling away, and every now and then, we could understand a snippet of what she was saying.

"They've landed," she muttered. "And they have finger-nails. Run for your lives."

People on one of the tourist trams noticed us and started to wave.

"Can you drive faster, Luis?" I asked. "This isn't the time for autographs."

"Why not?" Cassidy said. "My fans love me."

"Because your mother here is passed out like a sack of potatoes, and she needs medical attention," Luis said. "You ever think of that?"

"Why would I? My mother always said fans come first."

"Whoa, that's harsh, Cassidy."

"Don't pay attention to her," I said. "You're not really talking to Cassidy."

"Looks like her. Sounds like her. It must be her."

"The Supreme Leader from my planet has arrived on Earth and taken over her mind."

"You can't be serious, dude."

"It's Mr. Hitchcock," I said. "He's not really a director. He's the Supreme Leader in disguise."

"I thought that guy was too weird to be real," Luis said, turning abruptly down a small alley to avoid another flock of tourists. "And his crazy bird freaks me out too."

"That parrot is Citizen Cruel. He transformed her, but underneath those feathers still beats her mean alien heart."

"Let me guess. You told Delores who they really are, and she passed out before you could finish."

"No, I told her the whole story. I told her I was an alien too."

"He transformed right in front of her," Cassidy said, "but he got stuck at the head. And that was all she needed to see."

"My sensory enhancer didn't help," I added. "When she saw that it wasn't operated by batteries, she fell over like a tree."

"It wants to take over my bathtub," Delores muttered. Her mouth hung open and her head flopped around as we bumped along the path.

"Does this thing go any faster, Luis?" I asked.

"It's not exactly a Corvette. I've got the pedal to the metal, so this is it. The infirmary is right there on the other side of the dinosaur lake."

We sped past the huge *Jurassic World* attraction, where people were happily screaming as they careened down the steep water ride. It was strange that they were having so much fun while we were trying to deal with a mind-controlling evil dictator. I felt like we were actually experiencing a clash of two worlds. Hollywood versus the galaxy!

We pulled up to a little gray bungalow tucked down a dead end on the other side of the ride. The sign in front said INFIRMARY, NURSE ON DUTY.

"How'd you know this was here?" I asked Luis.

"Oh, I know the nurse, Lisa. She saved my life once, or at least my nose. I wanted to get her phone number, but I was too shy to ask her."

"What was wrong with your nose?" Cassidy asked.

"My buddy, who played Woody Woodpecker on the tour, got sick and they needed me to fill in. When I put the costume on, Woody's beak kept scraping against my nose. By the end of the day, my honker was so swollen it looked like an elbow. Lisa gave me ice and then a nose cast."

"Too bad it didn't improve your looks," Cassidy said.

There was just nothing nice going on in her brain. Every negative thought just came flowing out of her mouth with no filter.

Luis and I pulled Delores into a sort of upright position,

wrapping each of her arms around our necks, and dragged her inside the bungalow. Lisa was sitting behind a desk, talking on the phone. When she saw Delores, she hung up the phone immediately and motioned to a cot in an adjacent examining room. We plopped Delores down like a sack of avocados. "What happened to her?" Lisa asked.

"She fainted," we all said in unison.

"Oh, from the heat? Or lack of water?"

"Something like that," I said.

"She saw an alien," Cassidy blurted out. "And then hit the ground."

Lisa looked at me and nodded calmly.

"But we all know that's just a costume," she said. "There's no such thing as a real alien. By the way, I love your work."

"I'm an actor now too," Luis said. "Last time we met, I was Woody Woodpecker. You remember that?"

"That was an injury I'll never forget."

"Yeah, it was painful. But now I've turned in my beak, and I'm on *Oddball Academy*. You can see me tomorrow night, if you tune in."

Lisa smiled at him, and I think I saw her eyes twinkle. His twinkled back.

"Maybe I can get you a VIP pass to come sit in the audience tomorrow when we shoot the show," Luis said.

"Since when are you a VIP?" Cassidy snapped. "You've been a member of the cast for about three days, and by the way, you have the fewest lines of anyone."

"There are no small parts, only small actors," Luis said, giving Lisa a proud smile.

Cassidy cleared her throat.

"Uh . . . when you two are finished flirting, maybe someone could pay attention to my mother who's just lying there," Cassidy said.

"Of course," Lisa said. "Patients first."

Lisa took the stethoscope from around her neck and wrapped a blood pressure cuff around Delores's arm. We all waited nervously for the results, except Cassidy. She was scrolling through her phone.

"Oh no, I missed a call from Mr. Hitchcock," she said.

"Call him back right away," I said.

"Really? I thought you didn't want me talking to him ever again."

"I don't. But I need you to find out where he is."

"Why? What's it to you?"

"I have to talk to him right away. As soon as I know Delores is okay."

Lisa reached out and took Delores's pulse.

"Her blood pressure is fine, but her pulse is going very

fast," she said. "I think she had an anxiety attack. Did something scare her?"

"Maybe she saw a mouse," I said, a little too quickly.

"Or you," Cassidy said. "Anyone would faint at the sight of that face."

"Does she need to go to the hospital?" I asked Lisa.

"I could drive her there," Luis said. "Of course, her nurse would need to come. By the way, I have a hot car with a great sound system."

"I don't think she needs to go to the hospital," Lisa said. "I'll give her some fluids and let her rest. One of you should stay here."

"Cassidy, that's you," I said.

"Why me?"

"Uh, because she's your mother," Luis said. "And you're her daughter. Hello? Ring any bells?"

"All right," Cassidy sighed. "I guess I'm stuck here." Cassidy punched in a number on the phone. "Hi, Mr. Hitchcock," she said. "Bad news. I have to stay with my mom for a while. She's had some kind of panic attack, which is totally annoying. Yes, I know I'm a star, but sometimes even us stars have to deal with grunt work. Anyway, Buddy has ants in his pants and needs to see you right away. Okay, I'll tell him."

She ended the call and didn't say anything.

"Well?" I said. "Where is he?"

"He said to meet him at your spaceship on the back lot."

"You have a spaceship?" Lisa said with a laugh. "Your show must have a big prop budget."

The phone on the front desk rang and startled us all. Lisa left Delores's side to answer it, and from the other room, I could hear her saying, "Yes, he's here. I'll get him."

"Buddy, it's for you," she said, coming back into the examining room. "He says his name is Duane, and he doesn't sound very happy."

"Oh boy," Luis said. "We told him we'd be back in a half an hour it's already been twenty-five minutes."

Suddenly, Delores raised her head a little bit, and looked around. When she caught sight of me, she panicked.

"Where am I?" she said. "Did you take me to your planet? Have I been abducted?"

"You're in the infirmary at Universal Studios, ma'am," Lisa said. "On planet Earth."

"Watch out for him!" Delores screamed, pointing at me. "Get out while you can!"

"Maybe I should be the one to get out," I said. "I've got to see Mr. Hitchcock before we return to the set."

"I'm coming with you in case you need some protection," Luis said.

"Okay, we'll deal with Hitchcock and then get back to the set."

"All that in five minutes?" Luis said. "Impossible."

"Well, since you're such an alien," Lisa said with a little laugh, "maybe you can stop time."

"No, I tried that once when I was a kid, and I threw two of our moons out of orbit," I said. "The whole planet shook so much it made everyone nauseous. My grandma fixed it, but I got grounded for a whole month."

Lisa laughed out loud.

"You have such a great imagination," she said. "They should hire you to write the scripts, not just act in them."

"Our show is so weak, we barely have scripts," Cassidy said. "They must hire the writers straight out of kindergarten. That would be right at your level, Buddy."

I turned to Cassidy and just shook my head. Her eyes were so cold and had a faraway look.

"Cassidy, you're not yourself. Please don't do anything until you hear from me," I pleaded. "I'm going to see Hitchcock and fix everything. You'll be your old self again."

"You can keep my old self," she said. "I don't want it. This one is going places."

I saw Lisa shoot Cassidy a disapproving look. I couldn't

blame her. Cassidy was offending everyone she came in contact with. Her career and her personality were dissolving right in front of me.

The Supreme Leader was ruining not only my life, but my best friend's life. It was up to me to see if I could stop him. And I had five minutes to do it.

17

Luis and I dashed out of the infirmary and jumped into the golf cart. Luis drove like he was a race car driver, rounding corners on two wheels and yelling at people to get out of the way. We got stuck behind two crew members moving a grocery store set filled with plastic fruits and vegetables,

"Coming through! Clear Aisle Five," Luis shouted.

"Keep your socks on, kid. We'll move it as fast as we can."

The two guys pushed the whole set up against the sound stage wall, leaving a narrow path that didn't look wide enough for our cart to get through. That wasn't going to stop Luis.

"Hang on to your hat, Buddy, here we go."

"I don't have a hat," I pointed out.

"Fine, then hang on to your bald head, because we're going through no matter what."

Luis floored the accelerator and grabbed the steering wheel hard. I wasn't sure whether I should close all six of my eyes or keep them open. Either way, it was frightening. We made it through the narrow passage, but barely. My elbow bumped into a row of plastic bananas from the grocery set. You could hear them bounce on the asphalt.

"Hey, watch out, kid," one of the guys yelled. "Someone's going to slip on those."

"They're plastic," Luis shouted over his shoulder.

We headed up the hill to the back lot. Halfway up the hill, our cart slowed down to a stop and began rolling backward.

"You're going the wrong way," I said to Luis.

"No kidding, Sherlock," he answered. He reached for the emergency brake and we jerked to a halt.

"Why are you stopping?"

"Because one of us—I'm not naming any names, but he happens to have six eyes and red gums—forgot to plug in the cart at the infirmary. We're out of juice. Your body doesn't happen to generate any electrical power to charge up the battery, does it?"

"Don't be silly. I'm an alien, not a transformer."

"Then we'll have to use our feet. Can you make any time on those suction cups?"

"Yeah, I'll just tiptoe it. On my planet, I won a gold medal in the hundred-yard tiptoe dash. All my friends called me Toes."

"Okay, Toes," Luis said. "Let's see how fast you really are."

I took off and ran up the hill, with Luis panting behind me. He thought I was kidding about the gold medal, but I showed him. I was faster than the speed of light. Okay, not exactly that fast, but I definitely reached the spaceship well before him.

My spaceship had become its own little tourist attraction, so the theme park officials left it where I had landed. When I first came to Earth, I used to go there when I was homesick and just sit in the pilot's chair that Grandma Wrinkle designed for me. It made me feel close to her even though she was galaxies away. But in the past weeks, I had gotten so busy that I hadn't come to visit at all. My part had grown so much on the show that after rehearsals, it was all I could do to go home and submerge in a tub of water, pop a few avocados, learn my lines for the next day, and fall into bed.

When I reached the spaceship, I saw no one. Either the Supreme Leader wasn't there or he was hiding. It would be just like him to hide.

"Hello," I called. "Are you here?"

I waited in silence, and then I heard a squawking coming from behind me. I spun around to see a shadowy figure, with a bird perched on its shoulder, emerge from behind the rear fin of the spaceship. As he walked out of the darkness and into the fading light, I saw that he had abandoned his costume. This was no longer Mr. Hitchcock, but the Supreme Leader I had always feared, staring me down.

I refused to return his stare so that he couldn't do to me what he did to Cassidy.

"Look at me, Short Nose," he said.

"I won't," I answered. "I won't give you that opportunity. I've seen what you did to my friend, and I'm not about to

become your victim too."

"Your fate is in my hands now," he said. "You are small and I am all-powerful."

"You're all-powerful, Supreme Leader!" the parrot squawked.

"As soon as we deactivate your sensory enhancer," he went on, "you will once again be my subject and your disobedience will finally be over.

Oh, here comes your little human playmate, Zelda. We'll have to do away with him."

Panting from the exertion of the uphill run, Luis arrived at the spaceship. When he saw the Supreme Leader, he let out a gasp and a scream at the same time. You couldn't tell whether the air was going in or out of his lungs, but his body was definitely in a state of shock.

"Whoa, I've seen gross dudes before, but this guy wins hands down," he said.

"This guy," I said, "is the Supreme Leader of my planet."

"And don't you forget it," the leader said. "I'm taking this insolent subject, who made the deadly choice to disobey me, back to our planet to meet his fate."

"You're not taking Buddy anywhere, unless you want to deal with me," Luis said, rising up to his full height. The Supreme Leader was not impressed, height-wise or otherwise.

"Zelda," he said. "Deal with him."

The parrot spread her wings and her golden eyes flashed.

"I've been waiting!" she squawked.

She flew into the air and headed straight for Luis, her sharp talons aiming directly for his chest. Luis held up his arms to block her attack, but she beat her wings furiously so he couldn't see what was happening in front of him. Then she

dug her claws into his fore-arms and started pecking at his face.

"Ow!" he screamed. "Get off me!"

"Never!" the bird cackled with a laugh that sounded like she was chok-ing on a chicken bone. I would never forget that laugh. It was Citizen Cruel at her worst.

I heard the sound of a vehicle, and to my relief, turned to see the last tram of the day approaching. This would surely save us.

"Oh, look," I heard the tram driver say into his micro-phone. "We're in luck. They're rehearsing an *Oddball Academy* action sequence right now. I've never seen a parrot fight before, but movie magic is a constant surprise."

I waved my arms frantically at the driver.

"Over here!" I screamed. "The evil Supreme Leader has invaded, and his fierce parrot is attacking us."

"Sounds great," the driver said. "Keep up the good work. Folks, I'll bet we can all hardly wait to see that special episode they're doing this week. So long, Buddy. See you on TV."

My heart sank as he drove away and disappeared down the hill to drop the tourists off at the parking lot.

The battle between Luis and Zelda escalated to the point that the bird was attacking his eyebrows and pulling them out one hair at a time.

"Not my eyebrows!" Luis screamed. "They're very sensitive to pecking!"

There was such pain in his voice, and I could see some blood trickling down his forearm where Zelda had dug her talons into his skin. She was not about to stop her attack and Luis was close to helpless.

"Please make this stop," I cried to the Supreme Leader. "He's hurt."

"All you have to do is come back with me," the Supreme Leader said, "and I will release both your friends. His pain will stop and Cassidy's personality will be restored. Simply agree to return with me."

"No way," I said.

I knew I could not agree to that, but still, I had to do something. I let out a battle cry like actors in movies do when they are about to attack the enemy, and I lunged at Zelda, flinging the entire weight of my body at her. Her powerful wings battered my face and head, pushing me away like I was just a buzzing mosquito. I had to find another way to attack—but how?

I set my brain to super speed mode and replayed all the battle scenes I had ever seen from the thousands of movies Grandma Wrinkle and I had watched in her underground secret cave. In every one, the winning army had the high ground. That was the answer—I had to attack from above!

I jumped onto the side of the spaceship, attaching my suction cups to the shiny metal. One step at a time, I climbed higher and higher up the metallic ship until I was at eye level with the parrot. I put my suction cups into grip mode so they held me firmly in place. I reached out with the full length of my body, suspended in the air like a trapeze artist, and tried to grab Zelda from behind. I was able to wrap my arms around her feathery body and pull her off Luis.

"I've got you," I yelled at her. I felt so powerful and strong. For about two seconds, that is.

Then, with a surge of super cosmic strength, Zelda batted her wings with the force of a rocket engine. Just the wind her wings created ripped my suction cups right off the side of the spaceship and I fell to the ground.

I landed with a thud, and everything went black.

18

When I woke up, I found myself inside my spaceship, strapped into the passenger seat. My arms and legs were tied to the seat with Kapton tape, a super strong adhesive from my planet. I had used it to repair an injury that had almost ripped my body apart just a few weeks before, so I must have left it lying on the floor of the ship. The Supreme Leader had obviously found it and used it to restrain me. And once you're restrained with Kapton tape, there is no wiggle room.

My vision was blurry from my fall, but as the world came into focus, I saw six cold eyes, dark as charcoal, staring into mine. There was no light in those eyes, only gloom and menace.

"Did you have a nice rest?" the Supreme Leader inquired, never taking his eyes off mine.

"I wasn't resting. I was passed out."

"Just from that little fall?" he said with a smirk. "I thought you were a tough guy. But now I see you're just a little, puny thirteen-year-old with a traitor's heart and a weak body."

"I'm not the traitor—you are." I had no fear of speaking my mind. "You betrayed your people. They elected you to lead them, and you abused your power. You took away all their freedom and turned them into robots who are just there to serve you. That's not leadership. That's dictatorship."

"Thank you for the history lesson," he said, "but in this case I write the history, not you. So now I'm going to convince you to see the world as I do. All you have to do is look deeply into my eyes and submit to the thoughts I plant in your measly little brain. And if you don't, I will destroy you and your earthling friends. It's up to you."

I struggled to get free so I could escape his glare. But the Kapton tape held me so tightly that I couldn't move an inch.

When he began to speak and tried to place his thoughts inside my mind, I hummed loudly to drown out his words, but he raised his voice to such a high pitch that it penetrated my ears and shot directly into my brain.

"You regret ever having left our planet," he droned. "You will return with me and forever be obedient. You will be under my control and never again have a thought of your own."

I could feel the power of his words as if they were spikes being hammered into my mind. They were like molten lava seeping into every crevice of my brain. I had to block them from entering, so I started to sing. The problem was, I don't know any songs. And I have a horrible singing voice. Our vocal chords are short and produce a raspy squeaking sound when we try to carry a melody.

"You sound like a dying dung beetle," the Supreme Leader scoffed. "I know what you're trying to do, and it won't work."

Then I had an idea, a great idea, if I do say so myself. I could distract my brain from his awful words by filling it with my own words, words that I learned from the movies I have loved. I focused on those movies. I saw the characters and heard the words and let them wash over me like a beautiful river. And before I knew it, those words were in my mouth, and I was shouting them at the top of my three lungs.

First there was the would-be boxer working on the waterfront from that old black-and-white movie that was Grandma Wrinkle's favorite. "*I could have been a contender,*" I shouted. "*I could have been somebody, instead of a bum which is what I am.*"

Then the little mermaid with her shining red hair splashed into my head. "*I just don't see how a world that makes such wonderful things could be bad!*" I yelled.

The Supreme Leader realized what I was doing and raised his voice to an even higher pitch.

"Quiet, Citizen Short Nose," he commanded. "You will say goodbye to Earth and never think of it again. You are mine forever."

His words pushed the Little Mermaid even further under water, but I reached deep into my memory and conjured up the noble figure with his head held high and his arms crossed on his chest saying, "*Wakanda forever!*"

And then came the astronaut who spoke to the rocket scientists and said, "*Houston, we have a problem.*"

The astronaut's voice was strong, until he was replaced

in my mind by the sad southern woman who said "*I have always depended on the kindness of strangers.*"

And then . . . boom! . . . Wreck-It Ralph came swinging into my brain on a ball and chain yelling, "*There's no one I'd rather be than me.*"

It was wonderful and amazing that these great moments from movies were embedded so deeply in my memory and were all there when I needed them.

"What are you doing?" the Supreme Leader shouted. "I've never had so much resistance. Your mind isn't allowing my suggestions to enter. And it's filled with nonsense!"

"That isn't nonsense," I said. "It's movies, stories that enrich your life and make you feel everything."

"Stop thinking about them," he commanded. "You're blocking my thoughts. You're not like your friend Cassidy. She was easy to influence."

"I won't stop," I shouted. "You will never have my mind or my spirit."

The Supreme Leader backed away from me and let out a growl of frustration. He ripped off his leather gloves without even opening the snap and threw them on the floor of the spaceship.

"You leave me no choice but to resort to my secret weapon," he snarled. "This will break you for sure."

He snapped his arm out in front of me and pulled up his sleeve to reveal his holographic watch. Most people have those on my planet, but his was bigger and more advanced than the average citizen's. The face was made of a glowing crystal that spun around like a gyroscope and emitted a green light that grew darker and darker as it spun faster and faster.

"Bring her to me now!" He spoke into the face of the watch, the green light making his black eyes shimmer with an eerie glow. A form started to emerge from the depths of the crystal, twisting and turning and eventually taking on a lifelike shape. I heard a voice coming from the form and recognized it immediately. It was Grandma Wrinkle.

"Get your hairy paws off me, you bulky hunk of nothing!" she said.

Oh yes, that was Grandma Wrinkle, all right.

Gradually, her body took on dimension and began to appear out of the mist. I could see that she was struggling against someone trying to force her to be still.

"Grandma Wrinkle!" I called out. "It's me."

Suddenly she stopped struggling and turned toward my voice. Just seeing her face made me want to cry.

"Grandson, is that you?"

"It's him, all right," the Supreme Leader said, "and if you

ever want to see him again, you'd better convince him to come home."

"How are you, Grandson?" she asked. "Oh, how I long to see your face."

"I'm over here," I said, "in the passenger seat."

She knew exactly where to look, having built the spaceship herself. Her eyes tracked left, but it seemed like she was looking right over me.

"Can you fix it so she can see me?" I asked the Supreme Leader.

"Why would I do that?" he responded. "I'm not here for a family reunion. I manifested her to talk sense into you, and your job is to shut up and listen."

Then, turning to the image of Grandma Wrinkle, he said to her, "Talk. And make it convincing."

"Listen to you," Grandma Wrinkle said to the Supreme Leader. "Can't you hear what you've become? You're not the person I once knew so long ago. When we were in school together at Red Planet University, you were just Citizen Clumsy, a kind and intelligent person who tripped so much we all thought your legs were tied in a knot."

"Who's we?" he snapped. "Name names and I'll take care of them when I return."

"Wait a minute," I said. "You two knew each other? And were actually friends?"

"More than friends," Grandma Wrinkle said.

"Eeeuuuww," I said before I could stop myself. "Too much information."

"It's none of your business anyway," the Supreme Leader said. "That was long ago, and there is no trace of Citizen Clumsy left in me."

"I don't believe that," Grandma Wrinkle said. "He must be in there somewhere, the person who laughed so hard at *Hot Shots from Outer Space* that your popcorn flew all over the place."

"Popcorn is illegal," he said. "We only eat nutritional wafers."

"It's illegal because of you. You outlawed everything that tasted good, that smelled good, that sounded good. Remember music? And Earth rock and roll? You wanted so badly to dance, but you had two left feet and no jitter in your bug."

"My bug jittered fine," he answered, obviously angry. "You weren't exactly graceful yourself."

"I remember that time at the Saturn Club when everyone on the dance floor stopped and formed a circle around you." Grandma Wrinkle went on. "Your legs and arms went in four different directions at once."

"I was freestyling," he said.

"Oh, is that what you called it? It looked like you had gotten stung by a hive of hunchback sand hornets."

I couldn't believe what I was hearing. If I could, I would have taken my ears off and shaken them to make sure they were working. Grandma Wrinkle had gone on dates with the Supreme Leader? My mind was blown. Maybe there was a beating heart inside him after all.

But the next minute I found out that there was no such thing. Any twinkle that had been in his eyes disappeared, and his voice turned icy cold.

"Don't let this little walk down memory lane fool you," he said to me. "If you refuse to come home, I will do away with your precious grandmother."

"You would kill her?" I shuddered.

"Perhaps not," he said. "But I wouldn't think twice about sending her into endless orbit."

"Grandson, you must do what your heart tells you to do," Grandma Wrinkle said. "I have had rich and exciting experiences over my many hundreds of years. Your life is just beginning. You mustn't be concerned about me."

The Supreme Leader flashed a mean, crooked smile.

"But let me remind you," he said, tapping my chest hard with his pointed fingernail. "Endless orbit is not comfortable. It's cold and dark in deep space. There is hunger and fear and infinite loneliness. And one more thing, in case you're still trying to decide: You might want to look out the window."

I was able to turn my head just enough to see out of the

port hole. Luis was lying on the ground, passed out cold. Standing next to him was Cassidy, with Zelda perched on her arm. She was petting the bird's feathers. The Supreme Leader tapped on the window and beckoned her to come up the ladder and open the hatch of the spaceship. Cassidy stuck her head in and gasped when she saw the holographic image of Grandma Wrinkle, but she had nothing nice to say to her.

"Whoa," she exclaimed. "You have more wrinkles than an elephant's ankles. You should think about using a moisturizer. Or get a facial or something."

"Cassidy, that's really mean," I gasped. "Grandma Wrinkle is 987 years old."

"As if I couldn't tell," she snapped.

"I brought Cassidy here so you could clearly see your choices, Citizen Short Nose," the Supreme Leader said. "You can stay here on Earth and continue your fun little life, in which case, Cassidy will stay under my control and your grandmother will be sent into an endless orbit of darkness. I will destroy both of their lives. Or you can return with me, in which case, I will restore Cassidy to her original self and keep your grandmother on the planet."

An evil smile crossed his lips.

"So tell me, what's it going to be?"

19

agreed to return to my planet.

20

The Supreme Leader untaped me and we crawled out of the spaceship. Luis had regained consciousness but was still lying on the ground. Zelda was sitting on his chest, pecking at his head.

"Where's Cassidy?" I asked. I was so afraid the parrot had done something awful to her.

"Delores came in a golf cart and picked her up," Luis said. "She was giving Cassidy a hard time for leaving her alone in her time of need."

"Was Delores all recovered?"

"Oh yeah, definitely. She gave me a mouthful too. But Cassidy gave it right back to her. It wasn't pretty. You could hear them yelling all the way down the hill."

I breathed a sigh of relief. At least Cassidy was still alive and going home to safety.

"Quiet, you two," the Supreme Leader commanded with

authority. "Stop your meaningless chatter. I have, shall we say, persuaded Short Nose here to come back with me to our planet."

"What took so you long?" Zelda squawked.

"Silence, you mangy fowl!" he shouted. "I don't answer questions from underlings or lower life forms, especially incompetent ones like you. Don't forget, I had to finish the job you couldn't do."

"No, Buddy!" Luis said, struggling to his feet. "Tell me it isn't true. Tell me you didn't agree to return to your planet with that monster."

"I gave him no choice," the Supreme Leader said with sneer. "At first, his mouth was out of my control. He kept rambling about a Wakanda, whatever galaxy that's in. I had to involve his grandmother to silence him."

"You mean your former girlfriend," I said.

"You worthless traitor!" he shouted, poking me so hard in the chest with his long, sharp finger-nails that he broke the skin and a drop of purple blood oozed out. "From this moment forward, you will do what I ask, without question. I might not control your mind, but I will certainly control your actions."

"What are you going to do with him?" Luis asked. "Buddy, this dude could destroy you."

"If I don't go, he'll destroy my grandmother. And Cassidy too."

"Is there anything I can do to help you?" Luis asked. There was panic in his voice.

The Supreme Leader laughed. "What could *you* possibly do to thwart *me*? I am strong and you are weak."

"Oh yeah?" Luis said, flexing his impressive muscles so they danced up and down. "Get a load of this. You call that weak?"

"I call it foolish, you stupid human."

"What happens now?" I asked the Supreme Leader.

"Now we leave."

Luis gasped and ran toward me.

"No, Buddy!" he shouted. "I won't let you do this to yourself!"

"Zelda, take care of this pathetic outburst," the Supreme Leader commanded.

The parrot took off and shot like an arrow over to Luis's

shoulder. Then she let loose a giant watery bird poop that landed on his neck and slid all the way down his back.

"That is so gross!" Luis screamed. He tore off his shirt, ripping through each button until he was only in his tee shirt. "This was my favorite shirt," he yelled. "It cost me half a week's paycheck."

The parrot laughed wildly, and the raspy sound of choking on chicken bones echoed through the night.

"All aboard," the Supreme Leader said, grabbing me by the wrist and jerking me toward his spaceship. "Allow me to show you to your seat."

"Don't push me around," I said. "I'll come with you. I won't go back on my word. But I have a request. Give me twelve hours here on Earth. That's all I ask for."

"Why would I give you that?"

"Because I need to say goodbye to a lot of people here."

"What do I care about your wimpy little goodbyes?"

"Once I say a final goodbye, I'll be just a memory to these humans, and they will never follow me or bother us again."

Of course I didn't tell him the real reason why I wanted those twelve hours, but secretly I had a plan, a hope, a wild and crazy dream that in those hours, perhaps I could change his mind.

He agreed to let me stay for eight hours but not a second more.

My mind raced as I put together my plan on the spot. There was a lot to do, and I only had eight hours. The sun was going down behind the mountains, casting a purple glow on the now-empty back lot. The sunset made me even more aware that the clock was ticking.

"Luis, toss me your phone," I said.

"Are you going to call Duane and explain why we never showed up?"

"We can't deal with him right now. He's probably so furious he wouldn't hear my explanation anyway. Just give me the phone."

Luis threw it to me and I starting punching numbers wildly but nothing happened.

"You have to put my password in," Luis said. "It's guacamole427."

Of course it was.

My hands were shaking as I tried to put in the characters of his password. Why did it have to be so long?

"I gave you eight hours on Earth," the Supreme Leader said. "Are you going to use the whole time trying to make a phone call? That little human invention is so primitive."

"That's not primitive," Luis complained. "That's the newest phone out there. Got all the bells and whistles."

"In my world, all we need to do is visualize the person we want to speak with, and they instantly appear on our wristwatch. You people are light-years behind."

"Literally," I threw in.

I finally got the password entered and punched in the number.

"Barbara Daniel's office," the voice said.

"This is Buddy Burger. I need to speak with Ms. Daniel right away."

"I'm sorry, Mr. Burger. She's in a meeting."

"You have to interrupt the meeting and tell her this is urgent. It's an emergency."

"Okay, I'll see what I can do."

While I waited, I glanced at the Supreme Leader, who had started to pace in front of the spaceship. The parrot was sitting on his shoulder, clicking her tongue against her beak. While he paced in a perfect circle, he clicked his nails together impatiently. Between the two of them, it was a symphony of clicking.

"Buddy?" It was Ms. Daniel's voice on the phone. "What's wrong?"

"Nothing is wrong. Correct that. Everything is wrong. Listen, Ms. Daniel, I don't have time to explain, but I need a huge favor from you."

"Are you in danger?"

"No. Correct that. Yes."

"Dude, make up your mind," Luis said, shaking his head. "Spit it out."

I didn't want to reveal my plan in front of the Supreme Leader or give him a reason to read my mind, so I turned my back and took a few steps away.

"Here's what I need," I whispered to Ms. Daniel. She listened, and said she'd try.

When I hung up, I threw the phone back to Luis.

"Okay, here we go," I said. "Everyone come with me."

"Perhaps you've forgotten," said the Supreme Leader. "I don't follow you. You follow me."

"I think you're going to like what I have to show you," I said to him.

"You have no idea what I'm going to like," he exploded. "You can't begin to know what's in my mind."

"I'll take that chance," I said. "You promised me eight hours, and then I'll be yours forever. So please, let's just get in the golf cart."

Then I had a brilliant idea.

"You know what?" I said to the Supreme Leader. "You should drive."

"This little thing?" he said. "I pilot supersonic spaceships, not toys on four rubber wheels like this."

"Just try it," I said, sliding into the passenger seat. "It's fun."

He took the wheel and handed Zelda to Luis, who was sitting in the back seat.

"Hey, bird," Luis said, sliding over to one side. "Let me know if you still have a stomach problem."

"*Squawk!* I have a *you* problem!"

The Supreme Leader sat in front of the steering wheel and looked for a dashboard. "How do you start this thing?"

"Press your foot on the long pedal," I instructed him.

He did and we lurched forward in a sudden burst of motion.

"Brake!" I yelled.

"What?"

"Press the smaller pedal on the floor."

I heard his suction cups pop off the floor and hit the

brakes. We jerked to such a hard stop that Zelda slid all the way over to Luis and landed in his lap.

"Slow down," Zelda squawked. "I'm going to throw up."

"On no you don't," Luis said. "Get back on your own side and keep your stomach to yourself."

"Quiet!" the Supreme Leader snapped. "I don't need a backseat bird driver."

"You'll get the hang of it," I said to him. "Be gentle with the pedals. Just drive, and I'll tell you where to turn."

He put his foot on the accelerator and we took off down the hill, heading toward the sound stages. As we picked up speed, the golf cart started to swerve from one side of the road to the other. It was anything but a straight line.

"Keep your eyes on the road!" I yelled.

"Which ones?"

"All six of them."

He swiveled two of his eyes from the back of his head to the front.

"Oh," he said. "That makes a big difference."

We continued down the hill, but he was still driving like a maniac. I had the feeling he was secretly having fun.

At one point, we got so near the edge of the road that I thought we were going to run right off it and roll down the hill.

"Turn the wheel!" I shouted at him.

Just in the nick of time, he grabbed the steering wheel hard and we careened in the opposite direction, heading across the road toward the machine shop where all the props are built.

"Turn the wheel again!" I shouted, and we just narrowly missed plowing head on into the building.

To my surprise, the Supreme Leader let out a yelp. It wasn't a yelp of fear. It was a yelp of pleasure, the kind of yelp you make when you're barreling downhill on a roller coaster. We don't have roller coasters on my planet, or any amusement parks for that matter. The Supreme Leader had made all amusement off limits. And there he was, driving a golf cart like a crazy man, enjoying exactly what he had outlawed.

Fun. That was Step One of my plan.

To begin Step Two, I had him drive us to a building where there are several executive screening rooms. Those are small, deluxe theaters that the studio executives use to screen their finished movies, and Ms. Daniel had arranged for me to have one to myself for a few hours. We were greeted by a woman who was dressed all in denim, from her jacket and pants to her blue sneakers.

"Hi," she said. "I'm Jenna. I just got an urgent call from the head office that I'm to run a particular movie for you folks. I had to search hard for it, but I finally found it in our library. Come inside and I'll set it up for you."

As we climbed out of the golf cart, Jenna took a second look at us.

"You guys must've come directly from the set," she said.

"Why would you say that?" the Supreme Leader asked suspiciously.

"I assume that's a costume. If not, then I'm getting out of here." Jenna laughed and opened the door. "Make yourselves comfortable. And feel free to take some refreshments."

Jenna gestured to several rows of big, overstuffed leather chairs that looked so comfortable, you could sleep in them. On a counter nearby was a popcorn machine and shelves of every kind of movie candy you could imagine. I strolled up to the candy counter with the Supreme Leader right behind me.

"Don't ever turn your back on me," he said. "You're my prisoner and I'm watching you closely."

"Why don't you try a nice box of Junior Mints," I suggested. "They will melt in your mouth and they're easy on the gums.

I took a box for me and handed one to him. I sliced open the top with one of my long fingernails, and the minty aroma wafted up to my nose.

That was all my sensory enhancer needed. I could feel it starting to wiggle on my back, and I even heard a few soft snorts. It was preparing for action.

"Open mine too," the Supreme Leader commanded.

I opened the top and watched his reaction as the delicious fragrance overtook him. His sensory enhancer, which had been inactive for such a long time, got one whiff of the mint and the chocolate and went into instant overdrive. It shot over his shoulder, reached for the box, and dumped all the candy into its snout. Emitting wild sounds of enjoyment, it started to air dance with abandon, shaking with such force that it took the Supreme Leader with it. It looked like he was dancing with himself.

"Hey, you got some nice moves there," Luis said.

I'm not sure, but I think I may have detected the slightest touch of a smile on the Leader's red lips. When he noticed me watching him, he stopped dancing and immediately issued a stern command.

"Give me another box immediately," he ordered. "Hurry up and open it."

I opened a fresh box, and he took a few of the mints in his hand. His sensory enhancer dove for them, but he was quick, dropping a few in his mouth and pushing the greedy

sensory enhancer away. I could see his eyes light up as the mints melted in his mouth, waking up taste buds that had been asleep for years.

"A lot better than the nutritional wafers you require all your citizens eat," I commented. He didn't respond. He was too busy gumming down the whole box.

"You think those are good, wait until you try peanut butter cups," Luis said. "Your head will explode."

"Take a seat, folks," Jenna said over the intercom. "The show is about to start."

The Supreme Leader grabbed about six more boxes of Junior Mints. Zelda, who wanted to do everything that he did, helped herself to a box of popcorn. The Supreme Leader took his seat, and she flew after him, carrying the box in her beak. As they settled into one of the big, plush chairs, Zelda cackled with delight as she pecked away the popcorn.

While we were waiting for the movie to start, Luis grabbed my arm and pulled me aside.

"Dude, what are you doing?" he asked. "I don't get this whole thing."

"I have a plan," I whispered. "I believe, that way down deep, the Supreme Leader is a good guy, that his heart is different from what he shows the world."

"I don't know what you're seeing, but I'm seeing a dangerous, destructive creep with no heart at all."

"My Grandma Wrinkle would never have been friends with him if he was truly all bad. I bet he was once a different person and maybe even a lot of fun. Then something happened, and he got corrupted by power and all his good stuff got buried. My plan is to unbury it, peel him like an onion, and bring out who he used to be."

"Good luck with that!" Luis said.

"Citizen Short Nose," the Supreme Leader called out. "Stop that chattering and get over here next to me. Don't forget, I'm watching you with all six eyes."

"You're going to need some of them to watch the movie," I said.

"Everyone ready?" Jenna said over the intercom. "I've never heard of this movie myself, so let's see what it's like."

The lights dimmed and we sunk into our comfortable seats. The screen started to flicker and the music swelled. And then the title came up: *Hot Shots from Outer Space.*

23

When the movie title appeared on the screen, the Supreme Leader stopped eating his candy and sat perfectly still. I watched his reaction from the corner of my eyes, especially eyeballs number five and six. *Hot Shots from Outer Space* was a really funny movie, with cool teenage aliens surfing all over the galaxy on solar streams of wind. There was lots of action and comedy, so of course Grandma Wrinkle would have loved it.

As we watched the movie, Zelda laughed so hard that her popcorn flew out of its box, shot up in the air, and spilled into the Supreme Leader's lap. The sound of her chicken-bone laughter was so loud that Jenna came on the intercom and asked, "Does someone in there need a cough drop?"

The Supreme Leader's reaction was fascinating. At first, I could see him trying not to laugh, actually covering his mouth with all fourteen fingers. But halfway through the movie, he couldn't contain it anymore and burst out with a laugh that seemed to come from all the way down at the bottom of his suction cups. It was an alarming sound and for a minute, I thought maybe he needed a cough drop too. It was only when I saw his shoulders shaking that I realized he was busting out in laughter.

I glanced over at Luis. Neither of us could believe what we were seeing. The guy was not only laughing, he was more than laughing. He was hooting. When he realized that we were looking at him, he got hold of himself, sat up straight, and plastered a scowl on his face.

In the last scene of the movie, the teenage aliens have to go back to their own planets to return to school. They gather together in a space circle and say goodbye, pledging to never forget the great friendships they formed. It was really sad, but in that wonderful-sad kind of way, when you want to laugh and cry at the same

time. I heard a little gurgle coming from Luis's direction, and looked over to see him wiping his eyes with the back of his hand. Then I heard another gurgle coming from the seat next to me and saw that the Supreme Leader was fighting off tears, trying to suppress the emotions that wanted to come out.

When the lights came up, I asked him what he thought of the movie.

"It brought back memories," was all he said.

That was at least a start. I had seen a little crack in his tough exterior—a whoop of joy in the golf cart, a slurp of pleasure at the candy counter, a belly laugh in the movie, and now a hint of tears. Could it be that my plan was getting to him, awakening the person he had been long ago?

There was only one way to tell. I had to hurry on to the next step of my plan. We had used up two of my precious eight hours, so I had to move fast.

We thanked Jenna and left the screening room. Zelda still had her box of popcorn in her beak and was nibbling the unpopped kernels at the bottom. Outside, as the night crew swept the streets to prepare for the next day's shoot, we stopped for a moment. I asked Luis if I could borrow his phone, and when he gave it to me, I dialed Cassidy's number and passed the phone to the Supreme Leader.

"Can you talk to her, please, sir?" I requested. I knew that Cassidy wouldn't talk to me, but she'd certainly take his call. He took the phone gladly—he didn't mind talking to her, because he wanted to make sure he wasn't losing his grip on her mind.

"Hello," I heard Cassidy say from the speaker phone. "Oh, Mr. Hitchcock, it's so great that you called. My mom has been really on me about hanging around with you. She wants to push you out of the picture, but I'm not going to let her do that, because I know that you're the one who's going to make me the biggest star in the world."

"Can you tell her you want her to come to the Silverlake Café with us?" I whispered in the Supreme Leader's other ear.

"Why should I do that?" he snarled.

"Because she's under your control and she'll do anything you ask her. I have a surprise there I want both of you to see."

"I'm weary of this wild-goose chase," he grumbled. "I don't know why I said yes in the first place."

"But you did," I pointed out. "And you keep your word. That's what great leaders do, right?"

"Don't tell me about leadership, you upstart. You couldn't lead an army of dung beetles up a hill of sand."

"Please, just ask her," I said.

He did and of course she said yes. We arranged to pick her up as soon as possible. She would deal with her mother, she said, who was still in bed recovering from her fainting spell.

Luis brought his car around, and when the Supreme Leader saw what a great-looking convertible it was, his eyes lit up.

"I don't know where we're going, but I really like getting there in this. I'll drive, and you'll give me directions."

Luis didn't budge from the driver's seat.

"Did you hear me? I'm driving. Move over."

"Sorry, dude. We've seen the way you drive, and it's not street safe. I don't want Muriel to wind up wrapped around a lamp post."

"Whatever that is," the Supreme Leader said.

"It's a tall lamp that lights up the streets," Luis said. "They're on posts all over the city."

"How primitive," the Supreme Leader said. "On my planet, we have hover lights suspended above our urban environments. No posts to wrap oneself around."

"Sounds cool," Luis said as the Supreme Leader and I climbed into the back seat. "No way to get dented by a hovering light."

We drove down Ventura Blvd. to Cassidy's house. The warm California wind blew in our faces and the stars were all out and doing their twinkling thing. The palm trees stood in black silhouette against the neon signs from the shop windows. It was a beautiful sight. The Supreme Leader put his head back and let the soothing breeze waft over him. I heard him sigh with a mixture of sadness and happiness.

Cassidy was waiting on her front porch, with her big purse slung over her shoulder.

"Where are we going in such a giant hurry?" she asked.

"I granted your friend here eight hours to remain on Earth," the Supreme Leader said. "He's wasted several already, and apparently, the few more hours he has to waste involve you."

"To do what?" she asked, eyeing me suspiciously.

The Supreme Leader reached out and touched her arm, locking his dark eyes onto hers. I could see a little shudder run up her arm.

"Get in, Cassidy, and let's get this over with," he commanded.

"Yes, sir. Whatever you say," she answered.

"Floor it, Luis," I said as soon as Cassidy clicked into her seat belt. "I'm running out of time."

We made it to the Silverlake Café in record speed and

parked in front of the entrance. Luis put the top up and closed the windows. Even with the windows closed, you could still hear the music from the band that was already on stage. Zelda started to bob her head up and down in time to the beat.

"Where are we?" the Supreme Leader asked. "This noise makes my ears vibrate."

"This band's pretty loud," Cassidy explained, "but it's a really cool club. It's where Martha and I made our singing debut. I was great."

"That's why we're here," I said. "I want you to sing for Mr. Hitchcock. He's never seen that side of your talent."

"I thought you didn't approve of him," Cassidy said, "but whatever, I'm glad you changed your mind. I'll go ask the manager to let me perform. He won't say no to me, knowing how wildly talented I am."

She hopped out of the car and headed quickly toward the entrance. Luis opened his door to follow her when Zelda suddenly let out a squawk.

"What about me?" the parrot screeched, pressing her beak against the closed window.

"Sorry, no animals allowed inside," Luis said.

"*Squawk!* I'm not an animal, I'm Citizen Cruel."

"You look like a bird, you talk like a bird, you squawk like a bird, you fly like a bird, so I'm afraid it's a 'do not enter' for you," Luis said. He cracked a window for air. "State health laws say animals aren't allowed around food. Nothing personal, but you're not clean."

"*Squawk!* I'm very clean!"

"Yeah, well I got dirty shirt in the trunk of my car that says otherwise. Just stay here and finish your popcorn."

"Loser!" Zelda muttered as she perched on the steering wheel and buried her head into her popcorn box.

The Supreme Leader climbed out of the back seat, and I followed quickly. I took him by the arm to stop him before we went into the club. He reached down and coldly removed my hand from his arm.

"No one touches me unless I grant them permission," he said.

"I'm sorry," I said. "Humans are very touchy-feely, and I guess I've gotten a little that way myself."

"That is unacceptable," he said. "I promise you, we will erase all that when you return home."

"I just need to insist on one thing," I said. "I have to see that you have released Cassidy's mind before I enter the spaceship with you."

"I promised I would do that, and I will."

"No, I need to see you do it now. Give Cassidy her mind back, her own thoughts and feelings. She needs to be able to sing without your thoughts in her head. For her to sing well, she needs all her emotions—her own emotions."

"Why would she need that? Singing comes from the throat."

"No, not on this planet. Singing comes from the heart. And this will be the last time I'll ever hear her sing, so I want it to be great, something I'll never forget. And you'll find it interesting too."

"Human throat noises? Why would that interest me?"

"Maybe you'll see the power of music," I said, "how people melt when they hear it. You could take that knowledge back to our planet and use it."

"Hmmmm . . . use it," he murmured. Suddenly, I could see the wheels turning in his brain, but they weren't turning in the direction I had hoped.

"Yes!" he said. "Yes, yes, yes! I see what you mean. If I can understand how to control people's emotions with music, I could expand my powers. I'll have songs written about my greatness, songs to win people to my side. I will take over other planets. I will rule half the galaxy in no time. I will dominate the universe all through music."

He took my suggestion and went to the darkest part of

the dark side. But at least it was a way to get him to release his grip on Cassidy so he could hear her sing with all her heart. I was counting on that to do the trick.

We hurried inside the club, where Luis had gotten us a table for four, and Cassidy was talking to the manager. She came bounding over to us.

"It's all set," she said. "I explained that you two were still in costume from the show so he didn't freak out. And then I convinced him to let me go on right after this band is finished. He's fitting me in because I was such a knockout the last time I sang here. I'm going to remind everyone how great I was."

"Please don't do that," I said.

"Why not? Great is great, might as well call it what it is."

"Now is the time," I said to the Supreme Leader. "You can't let her go on stage and say things like that. The audience will turn on her. Please, do this for her."

"I won't do it for her, but I will do it for the chance at intergalactic domination."

He reached out and took Cassidy's hand in his.

"Look deeply into my eyes," he said, almost chanting. "Hear my voice and only my voice. I am going to allow you to be the Cassidy I first met. A happy young actress, full of positive energy, humble and thoughtful, who spreads joy everywhere. When you sing, you move people, lift their spirits to a higher place. For now, I am freeing you to do that."

He let go of her hand. Cassidy blinked hard, and I swear I saw her whole face change. The smile on her lips returned, her eyes twinkled, and her very skin seemed to relax.

"Hi, Buddy," she said as if she were seeing me for the first time in a long while. "You look cute."

My heart leapt up in my chest. There she was, my friend Cassidy!

"Go get 'em," I said to her. "Break a leg. Break lots of legs."

She grinned and bounded up the stairs to the stage, ready to make her entrance. The club manager was already introducing her.

"Hey, everyone, we have a surprise guest for you tonight. You know her from *Oddball Academy* and her recent appearance on *Star Roundup*. So give a warm Silverlake Café welcome for Cassidy Cambridge."

She walked up to the microphone.

"Boo!" shouted lots of people from the audience.

"You think you're so high and mighty!" a girl with red hair yelled.

When Cassidy heard the boos and the taunts coming from the audience, her face fell and her smile disappeared.

She looked so hurt and vulnerable. My heart broke for her. I saw her searching the audience for some support, and finally her eyes landed on all six of mine. I jumped to my feet and let out a massive cheer.

"We love you, Cassidy!" I whooped.

"Speak for yourself, weirdo!" a teenager from the front row answered.

I swiveled all my eyes over to him and glared. "Just give her a chance, will you? Come on, Cass. You can do this."

Cassidy took a deep breath and started her song. She had picked one of my favorites, a song she wrote herself called "My Best Friend." It starts slow and describes two best friends who have a huge fight. They think their relationship is over. When Cassidy sang that part, her voice was full of sadness. The audience settled down as soon as she began—her voice was lilting and sweet. Her emotions were real and pure. As she sang, I saw how she captured the audience. People grew peaceful and swayed gently in their seats. She had them in the palm of her hand. Even the teenager from the front row was enthralled.

Luis tapped me on the shoulder and whispered, "Check him out."

I glanced at the Supreme Leader, and he was gently swaying in his seat. That gave me hope.

Halfway through, the song takes a turn, and the two friends realize that their friendship is more important than any disagreement they had. As they make up and reunite, the music speeds up and develops a real thumping beat, which Cassidy pounded out by stomping her feet. Everyone started to clap in rhythm, and before I knew it, the Supreme Leader had jumped to his feet and was attempting to clap. I say "attempting" because he had trouble putting his hands together. I know from experience that clapping is hard when you have fourteen fingers. At least three of them are always in the way.

What happened next is a sight I will never forget if I live to be four thousand years old. The Supreme Leader started to dance—if you can call it dancing. His arms were going up and down, while his legs were going in and out. He twirled on his tiptoes in two directions at once, twisting himself into a knot, then spinning like a tornado. You could hear the popping of his suction cups in time to the music. Every now and then, one of them got stuck and would lift up a plank of wood from the floor. He'd kick it off and go right on spinning.

Members of the audience noticed him dancing. You'd have to be a lower life form with no eyes NOT to notice.

The kids formed a circle around him and watched as his movements got more and more intense. And weird.

Oddly, no one laughed.

"This guy's really feeling it," the teenager with the attitude said.

"You go, spaceman!" the girl with the red hair chimed in.

Before long, everyone in the crowd was clapping in rhythm, dancing in the circle, trying to imitate the Supreme Leader's moves. Cassidy was belting out her song onstage. People were clapping and hollering. And best of all, the Supreme Leader was whooping it up like a hot shot from outer space, laughing so hard that lavender tears sprang from every one of his eyes.

It was a sight to behold.

24

The dance party went on for hours, with everyone singing and dancing and hollering and hooting. The audience loved Cassidy and clearly forgave her for her brief journey into Jerk Land. But the person they really loved was the Supreme Leader. They wanted to dance like him and duplicated his every movement perfectly, except for the part where his suction cups ripped up the floor. They even picked him up and carried him on their shoulders, forming a conga line around the room with him trying to snap his fourteen fingers while they paraded.

As for the Supreme Leader, he seemed to be an entirely different person. I thought his face was going to crack from smiling. Streams of lavender sweat ran down his bald head into his eyes, but even that didn't stop him. He just danced by a pitcher of water on a table, and without missing a beat, poured the whole thing over his head to clear out his eyes.

What he didn't realize was that it wasn't water—it was a carbonated lemon-lime soda. When the bubbles hit his eyes, they spun around in crazy circles. I wish you could have been there to see what happened when the liquid dribbled from his eyes into his mouth. Both his tongues shot out past his lips. If they could talk, they would have shouted hallelujah!

Two hours later, the club manager finally said he was closing and we had to leave. Although I had a great time, I was glad the party was over, as I had used up another two of my precious hours. As people streamed out of the club, everyone said a sweet goodbye to the leader.

"Let's meet back here next week," the girl with the red hair said.

"That won't be possible," he answered. "I have to return to my planet."

"Cool," the girl laughed. "Maybe we'll meet up because I'm going to the moon in my rocket."

"The moon is not on my trajectory."

We were the last to leave. The cool night air felt good as we headed to Luis's car. Zelda was perched on the headrest, pressing her face against the window. When she saw us, she started to flap her wings and peck on the glass.

"What took so long?" she squawked.

"Fun takes time," the Supreme Leader said.

"Fun! Human fun?" she cackled.

"Yes," he said. "And plenty of it."

We climbed into our seats and Luis started the engine.

"Where to now?" he asked. I knew exactly what the next step of my plan was. It was time for the Supreme Leader and I to have The Talk.

"I'm hungry," I said. "I have a great idea. Luis, how late is your grandmother's restaurant open?"

"She closes up right after dinner. But if you want to go there, I know where the key is. And where the guacamole is."

"What is this guacamole you keep talking about?" the Supreme Leader asked.

"Just wait and see," I said. "Your tongues are going to love it."

Just as we were about to take off, Cassidy's phone rang. It was Delores, still sounding groggy, but definitely angry-groggy.

"Where are you, young lady?" she shouted into the phone. "It's way past your curfew. I'm worried sick. I was just about to start calling the hospitals to see if you had been in an accident."

"I'm sorry I made you worry, Mom," Cassidy said. "I'm

safe. I'm with Buddy and Luis, and we're just going to get something to eat."

"Oh no you're not. There's plenty to eat here," Delores said. "You need to come home now. And don't give me any of that salty new attitude of yours."

"No more salty attitude, Mom. That's gone. I'm me again. I'll explain everything when I see you. Just promise me that this time you'll listen."

"I'll try, Cassidy. Just come home."

Cassidy hung up the phone and turned to Luis.

"Can you drop me off at my house before you guys go to eat?"

"Sure thing, chicken wing," he said.

Luis put the top down and we drove to Cassidy's house. Before she jumped out of the car, she turned to me.

"Good night, Buddy. After I make up with my mom, I'm going to make up with Duane and everyone in the cast. Maybe they'll let me back on the show."

"I hope so," I said.

I couldn't bear to tell her that if my plan didn't work, I would have to return to my planet with the Supreme Leader. This might be the last time we'd ever see each other. Unaware of just how shaky our future together was, Cassidy slung her big purse over her shoulder and ran into the house. The last glimpse I got was of her and Delores hugging.

Luis, the Supreme Leader, and I drove over the canyon road that leads into the heart of Hollywood. As we climbed the hills, I looked out at the valley filled with twinkling lights from so many homes. I thought of the people inside, enjoying their families, reading bedtime stories, having a midnight snack. And that's where we were heading, for our own midnight snack. No matter what those families were having, I knew it couldn't beat Luis's grandma's guacamole and chips.

Her restaurant was tucked into a corner lot in Hollywood, marked by a neon sign that read LOS AMIGOS. There was a fountain in the courtyard and the rustic wooden door opening into the dining room displayed a hand-lettered notice that said CERRADO/CLOSED. Luis hurried to the wall next to the door and slid out a loose brick. The key was hidden inside. He held it up so we could see, then unlocked the door and flipped on the lights.

"*Bienvenidos*," he called. I ran that through my mental Earth dictionary and found that it meant "welcome" in Spanish. Also, I was finally able to learn one word in Hungarian. In case you're interested in how to say "welcome" in

Hungarian, it's *udvozoljuk*. Don't laugh—you never know when that might come in handy.

The Supreme Leader started to climb from the car, but quickly sunk back down into his seat.

"Suddenly, I'm not feeling well," he groaned.

"Let me guess. You feel light-headed, tired, weak, and shaky and everything from your knees down is numb."

"How did you know?"

"Been there, done that. And I know exactly what you need—hydration and some avocado. You used up a lot of your life force on the dance floor, and your body is saying, 'That's enough of that. Give me an avocado or three.'"

In making my plan, I hadn't predicted that the Supreme Leader would get sick, but it wasn't a bad thing. If I could help him feel better, he would trust that I was on his side.

I took his hand and helped him out of the back seat. He put a limp arm around my shoulder and hung on tight. As we left the car, Zelda started to flap her wings and squawk.

"You can't leave me here!" she complained. "Not again!"

"No animals allowed," I hollered behind me.

"But I'm Citizen Cruel!" she cackled. "Citizen Cruel! Citizen Cruel! Citizen Cruel!"

Her screeching voice echoed in my ears as we entered

the restaurant. The inside of Los Amigos was dimly lit with amber-colored wall lamps that cast an orange glow on the red-leather booths. Autographed framed black-and-white pictures of Hollywood celebrities lined the wall. I recognized so many of those famous faces from the movies and television shows Grandma Wrinkle and I had watched. There was Adam Sandler making a funny face, Oprah Winfrey looking all serious, and even a picture of the Fonz from a TV show we loved called *Happy Days*. He had both thumbs up and had written, "Grandma C, you make the best guacamole ever!"

As I helped the Supreme Leader to a booth, I could see that he was fading fast. Luis rushed into the kitchen and brought us several pitchers of water and whatever guacamole he could find in the refrigerator. I held one of the pitchers to the Supreme Leader's mouth.

"Drink up and keep going until it's finished," I said.

"I don't take orders from you." His voice sounded weak, but he was still holding on to his authority.

"Right now you do, because I'm holding the water. Trust me, this will help."

He took a few gulps and then grabbed the pitcher from me with both hands and drank the whole thing down.

"More," he said.

He went through six more pitchers of water in about ten seconds.

"Wow," Luis said. "I'm surprised you have room in your stomach for all that water."

"That's why we have two stomachs," I said. "More room to fill the tank. Let's move on to the guacamole and see if that works."

Luis took the tub of guacamole and the bowl of chips and placed them on the table in front of the Supreme Leader.

"*Disfruta la comida*," he said.

Once again, I had to consult my mental Earth dictionary and learned that he had said "enjoy the food." I also learned how to say "armadillos eat big ants" in Spanish, but since that didn't apply here, I just let it drift out of my head.

"Put a glob of that guacamole on a chip and shove it in your mouth," Luis instructed the Supreme Leader. "Can't beat it."

"No chips," I protested. "Don't forget, we have no teeth, and it takes a lot of energy to gum crunchy things and make them soft. He's got to go straight to the avocado. Go ahead, use your hands," I said, pushing the plastic tub up close to him. "It's not pretty but it will get the job done."

The Leader reached into the tub with both hands, and using all fourteen fingernails as spoons, devoured the entire contents like a vacuum cleaner sucking up dirt.

"More," he said.

"I don't know about that," Luis said. "There's one more tub left, but if we use that, my grandma won't have any to serve the customers tomorrow."

"Luis, this is an emergency," I argued. "You've seen me sick like this before, when avocados were the only thing that could bring me back to life. I'm sure your grandmother will understand."

"Oh right, that I gave the last bit of her guacamole to an alien dictator? She'll buy that one, for sure."

"Please go and get it," I begged. "If she gets mad, I'll take the heat."

"Oh really? Exactly how are you going to do that, Buddy? You're leaving to go back to your planet, remember?" Luis checked his watch. "Blast off is in two hours. Come to think of it, I'd better give your leader the rest of the guacamole. I want this guy alert when he's driving that spaceship. He could make a wrong turn at Jupiter and you could end up in a black hole."

Luis disappeared into the kitchen. The Supreme Leader turned his head, looking around the room as if seeing it for the first time. The water had given him some life force and the first batch of guacamole was beginning to do its job.

"I can feel my feet," he said.

"That's a good sign. Your life force starts in your feet and travels up to your brain. You're going to be okay."

Another sign that the Supreme Leader was getting his strength back was that his sensory enhancer had a little burst of energy and started to sniff the chips and the empty guacamole bowl. It poked its snout into a dish of salsa and let out a yelp of pain. It must've tried the extra-hot stuff.

Luis returned with the last batch of guacamole.

"Ah, straight out of Grandma's fridge," I said.

"Did you say something about your grandmother?" the Supreme Leader asked.

I had actually been talking about Luis's grandmother, but I didn't let him know that. I had been hoping the conversation would turn to my grandmother.

"Yes," I said. "I always think about my grandmother. She's never far from my mind."

"That's odd," he said, "because I've been thinking about her this whole night too. Whooping it up in the golf cart. Laughing in the movie. Driving in the warm breeze. Loving the music. Dancing until my feet felt like they had wings. She and I did things like that together when we were young."

There it was. There was the opportunity I had been waiting for.

"You can do all those things again," I said.

"Not possible," he answered. "They are forbidden."

"But you were the one who outlawed them, you and Citizen Shady, with your relentless need for absolute power. But you can change everything back to the way it was. Our planet could have beautiful colors and music and art and delicious food and all the wonders our senses bring us. You're the leader. It's within your power to restore what you've taken away."

"But the citizens will question my judgment. I will look like a weak fool."

"No, you will look like a strong hero. The citizens will celebrate. We will banish the memory of Citizen Shady and all that you and he destroyed."

The Supreme Leader sat there at the table, scratching his chin and thinking. I knew we were at a critical moment. This was the time for me to invoke the final step of my plan. I had shown him the possibilities of a new world order for our planet. Now that he was mulling over what he had lost, I had to get him to commit to change. There was only one person in the universe who could help push him over the edge.

"Let's conjure up Grandma Wrinkle," I said. "I want to tell her that I'm returning home. And that you're going to release her from her prison pod. You are, aren't you?"

"I keep my word," he said.

"She'll be glad to know that."

He held out his arm and spoke into the crystal of his holographic watch. "Get me prison pod 4372X," he said. The crystal began to spin, and a green mist spiraled upward and filled the restaurant with its glow.

"Whoa," Luis said. "You got some major special effects in that thing."

Within seconds, Grandma Wrinkle's form appeared. She seemed to be lying on the floor of her prison pod.

"What now?" she snapped, looking up. "You're inter-rupting my daily workout."

Slowly she became fully visible. I could see that she was on the ground, doing push-ups.

"Is she doing those one-armed?" Luis asked. "I can barely do four of those without falling on my face."

"She believes in staying physically fit," I said.

"Always did," the Supreme Leader chimed in. I detected a note of amusement in his voice.

"Grandma Wrinkle, I have good news," I began. "I'm coming home. We blast off in two hours."

Her reaction surprised me. I thought she'd be joyous, but instead, she cast a suspicious look.

"Let me talk with Citizen Clumsy," she said. "Where is he?"

"I'm right here," he said, putting his face in front of the hologram.

"This doesn't sound right to me," she said. "How did you convince my grandson to come back here? Did you threaten him? Did you say you were going to harm me? Don't you dare use me to get to him! I won't have it!"

"He's agreed to come of his own accord," the Supreme Leader said.

"How is that possible, Grandson?" Grandma Wrinkle said. "You left in order to experience life to the fullest with all your senses. What has he done to you? Are you ready to give that up?"

"Well, there's a possibility that maybe I won't have to," I said slowly, carefully watching the Supreme Leader's reaction. "Tonight, he and I had a great time together. It started simply enough with a movie, one the two of you saw together."

"*Hot Shots from Outer Space?*" she exclaimed. "Clumsy, was it as great as I remember?"

"Even better," he said, a smile cracking his lips. "I laughed so hard at the mini-Martian motorcycle chase and then cried my heart out during the surf circle when the hot shots all had to say goodbye."

"Did you say cry?" Grandma Wrinkle said. "Wait a minute. Did you say heart? I didn't think you still had one."

"He does," I said.

"I thought you lost it when you fell under the influence of that evil Citizen Shady. That man was as corrupt as they come."

"He was my mentor for all these years," the Supreme Leader said. "But—"

"But you're not all bad at the core," I interrupted. "I saw it with my own eyes. And you still have rhythm too. You should have seen him dance, Grandma."

"I have. Has he gotten any better?"

The Supreme Leader chuckled. "Well, my moves were still somewhat clumsy—"

"But everyone loved him anyway," I interrupted again. "They picked him up and carried him around the club and celebrated him because he was having the time of his life, whooping and laughing up a storm."

"Wait a minute. Did you say he laughed?"

"Until lavender tears rolled down his face," I said.

"Is that true, Citizen Clumsy?" Grandma Wrinkle asked. "Were you actually experiencing fun through the pleasure of your senses?"

"I couldn't believe it either," he said. "It was the best time of my life—except for the afternoon you and I ran down the sand dunes of Altomar and then plunged into the glowing rose-colored waters of Lake Titan."

Grandma Wrinkle actually giggled. "I'll never forget that day, but I thought for certain you had forgotten all about it."

"I had," he said. "But during these last hours on Earth, so much has come back to me. How the warm wind feels on your face, how the rhythm of music fills your body, how your stomachs hurt when you laugh too hard, how guacamole tastes so creamy and spicy on your two tongues."

"I was with you until the guac-a-what," Grandma Wrinkle said.

"Maybe I can bring some home," he said. "It's hard to describe in words."

"I'll get my grandma to whip you up another batch," Luis said.

"Grandma Wrinkle," I said. "Do you have anything to say to the Supreme Leader?"

"I do not," she said. "But I do have something to say to Citizen Clumsy. Come home, my friend. Turn the government back to the people. Release us to experience life to the fullest. You have tried your awful experiment in power, but it has created only unhappiness. Let us all have our lives back. Our full lives."

The Supreme Leader sat perfectly still. Luis and I barely breathed. There was not a sound in the restaurant except for the Supreme Leader's breath going in and out, in and out.

When at last he spoke, it was with a voice filled with infinite regret and quiet determination.

"You have brought my memory back to life," he said, putting his hand on my shoulder. "Thanks to you, I remember our world and what it was. It was beautiful, and I will make it so again."

"We will make it so again," Grandma Wrinkle said. "All of us, working together."

"Yes. All of us."

"Does that mean Grandma Wrinkle will be free?"

"Yes," he said. "She will be at my side. And you are free to stay here on Earth, as you wish. I will not pursue you. You have my word."

My heart jumped and did somersaults inside my chest.

This was everything I had hoped for.

Or was it?

25

We set the blastoff time for exactly 6:14 in the morning, the time that the sun was to rise over Universal Studios. No one would be on the back lot yet, not even the morning shift. Luis pulled his car up next to the Supreme Leader's spaceship, where it was hidden among some bushes. As we got out of the car, Zelda began to squawk.

"What about me! You're not going to leave me here," she cackled.

"Yes, I am," the Supreme Leader said.

"You can't be serious!"

"You have proven to be a complete failure," he said. "And furthermore, we are going to eliminate cruelty on our planet, so there is no need for you."

"Wait a minute," I said. "You're not going to leave Citizen Cruel here with me."

"Or me!" Luis said. "She and I don't get along. We are definitely not birds of a feather. And I have my ripped-up favorite shirt to prove it. Not to mention the bird-poop stain."

The Supreme Leader cleared away the bushes that were covering his spaceship. It was almost identical to mine, except it had a streak along the side that had his name emblazoned in gold letters.

"Do you need to put gas in this thing?" Luis asked.

"What a quaint question," he answered. "We haven't used gasoline for five thousand years."

"I bet you save a bundle on that," Luis said. "I spend half my salary filling up Muriel."

"You humans should know by now how dangerous fossil fuels are," the Supreme Leader said. "It took us a while, but we got there."

He looked up at his spaceship, then down at his wristwatch.

"I guess it's time for me to board," he said. I noticed that he was shivering in the morning cold.

"Wait a second," I said, and ran back to the car to retrieve my *Oddball Academy* sweatshirt that I keep in Luis's trunk. When I returned, I handed it to him. "Here's something to remember us by."

He slipped it over his bumpy head and burst out into a smile.

"How do I look?" he asked.

"Like a television star," I answered.

He turned to climb the stairs to the hatch. When he got to the top and opened the door, he looked back and let all six of his eyes take in the scene—the sound stages below, the mountains above, the Hollywood sign glimmering in the sunrise.

"I like this planet Earth," he said. "I learned a lot here. I have a big job ahead of me."

"You can do it," Luis said. "You're the man."

"I'm an alien."

"Hey, dude, that's twice as cool."

"Farewell, young friend," the Supreme Leader said to me. "I wish you well in your chosen life. You're fearless, and I admire that."

"I've learned to admire you too," I said. "It takes a lot of courage to change."

We were silent.

"I guess this is goodbye for us then," I said.

He nodded. Then without another word, he swiveled his eyes around and turned toward the hatch. I wondered if those eyes were filled with lavender tears that he was trying to hide. When I saw him lift his arm and wipe his eyes with his sleeve, I knew I was right. Then he disappeared into the spaceship.

"No! Don't leave me!" Zelda's squawk pierced the morning air. "You can't! Don't do it!"

Zelda threw herself on the ground at the foot of the ladder. She beat the pavement with her wings and kicked her claws in the air, like a two-year-old throwing a tantrum.

"Please! I beg you! Don't make me remain in this lowly life form forever. Don't leave me among these humans!"

Suddenly, the hatch swung open, and I could hear the Supreme Leader's voice.

"All right!" he sighed. "If I'm going to become Mr. Nice Guy, I might as well start right now."

Zelda took off like an eagle and swooped up to the door, squawking happily.

"Thank you, oh kind Leader! I will always . . ."

"Oh, shut up. Just sit down and put your seat belt on," he growled, slamming the hatch door closed.

We heard the metal lock of the door clang shut. The roar of the engines filled the air. Luis and I backed far away and stood watching as smoke and fire poured out of the rocket.

It felt like the earth under our feet was shaking as the spaceship blasted off into the sky above us and veered left toward the Milky Way on its journey to the red dwarf planet.

"So now what?" Luis asked when the rocket had become just a tiny, silver dart in the sky.

"We're professionals," I answered. "We have a special to film."

"Dude, I've got to go home and shower before I can put this face on TV."

"Me too," I said. "Isn't this a weird world? Doing intergalactic battle one minute and taking a warm shower the next. That's show business for you."

When Luis dropped me off at Cassidy's house, everyone was still asleep. I took a fast shower, climbed into my bed, and fell asleep like a bear in hibernation. I set my alarm for two hours, but I was so exhausted, I slept right through it and woke up at noon. I ran frantically around the house and saw that Delores and Cassidy were gone. There was a note on the kitchen counter from Cassidy that said, "At rehearsal. Wish me luck."

Fortunately, I was already in my alien skin, so all I had to do was call a car to take me to the studio. While I was waiting, I whipped up an avocado smoothie that would at

least give me a burst of energy and gulped it down on the way to the studio.

"Hi everyone," I said, as I rushed onto Stage 42 and made a beeline for the table where the revised scripts were waiting. The cast was already on the set, walking through the changes. I noticed immediately that Cassidy was in the scene. She flashed me a thumbs-up. I don't know what she had said to Duane to convince him to put her back in the show, but it had obviously worked.

"Well, look who decided to show up," Duane said. "Where were you last night? And this morning? Getting your alien beauty rest?"

"Sorry I overslept. We were out late and . . ."

"And man, you wouldn't believe what an incredible night it was," Luis said from his place on the locker room set.

"Much as we're all dying to hear about your social life, save it for another time." Duane held up his hand to stop any further explanation. "Open your script, Buddy, we're on page 23. As you can see, we went back to the earlier draft with Cassidy in it."

"Just give me one second." I held the script up to my forehead and let my brain absorb the fifty-four pages. It's a good thing I had that smoothie, because all my memory cells were working at warp speed.

"Got it," I said. "I'm ready to go."

"Sure, like you can read that fast." Tyler sneered.

"I took a speed-reading class once," Martha said. "It didn't work for me, but I learned to sing fast. You want to hear?"

"No," everyone said in unison.

"I can recite the Gettysburg Address in Lincoln's actual voice in just thirteen seconds," Ulysses said. "You want to hear?"

"No," everyone said again.

"Great!" he said and launched into it anyway. "Fourscore-andsevenyearsago . . ."

"We get the picture, little man," Tyler said.

"Really? Do you imagine my stovepipe hat too?"

"What I am imagining is the clock ticking," Duane said. "And that's not in our favor. The audience for the dress rehearsal arrives in three hours. And the final shoot is two hours after that. So we've got to hustle to get ready. All the network executives from Barbara Daniel on down are going to be here, so we have to be at our best."

"Don't worry, Duane," Cassidy said. "We're a great team. We always deliver."

"This is the least-rehearsed show I've ever done," he said. "I hope you're right, for all our sakes."

We worked without a break all afternoon, going over each scene twice. It wasn't the best dress rehearsal I'd even been part of. Not that I'd been part of that many, but this one definitely sucked lemons. Luis forgot his opening line, the lights on the spaceship didn't blink during the landing, Ulysses tripped over his untied shoelace, and Martha got a nosebleed when Ulysses plowed into her. But Cassidy and I were on our game . . . our chemistry was back on fire. I was so proud of her. Even after everything she had gone through in the last few days, she was able to put her mind on her performance and deliver her lines like the true professional she is. Even Delores, standing in the wings, couldn't find fault with her.

After the dress rehearsal, Duane gathered us together backstage.

"Well, that was definitely mediocre," he said. "There's an old saying in Hollywood that if the dress rehearsal is bad, the performance will be great. I'm going with that. Break a leg, everyone."

If I live to be two thousand and three years old, I will never ever grow tired of that expression. Every time I hear it, it tickles me right down to my suction cups. You humans sure like to make things complicated.

The old saying held true. Despite our terrible dress

rehearsal, we had a great performance in front of the real audience. Everyone in the cast got their lines right. The spaceship blinked on cue. Luis couldn't have been more charming, and even when he flashed a shy grin at Nurse Lisa in the audience, it seemed to fit right into the script. Tyler had his usual fan club in the front row, and he treated them to a flash of his pearly whites during breaks. Martha sang, Ulysses remained upright, Cassidy was her usual sweet self, and my sensory enhancer even responded appropriately for once. It only let out one small snort when it got a whiff of the fun-sized candy bars that they throw into the audience between scenes.

When the show ended, we all went backstage and high-fived each other. Duane came running back to congratulate us and did something I've never seen him do—smile!

"I really doubted you could do it," he said, "but you guys proved me wrong. You put on a great show. Come on out for your bows."

When we came back to the stage, the crew had rolled out a red curtain that stretched across the set. We all stood in front of it, held each other's hands, and bowed in unison. The audience cheered. We took a second bow, and they cheered louder. By the third bow, they were standing up, stamping their feet on the bleachers. Barbara Daniel, Chuck

Smeller, and a row of other young executives were applauding too. Even Delores, who had sandwiched herself between Ms. Daniel and Mr. Smeller, was grinning from ear to ear. From the corner of my eye, I saw Chuck Smeller reach into his pocket and hand Ms. Daniel a phone. She dialed a number, and then held up the phone so the person at the other end could hear the wild applause.

We took our final bow, and I stood there letting the sights and sounds of this joyous moment wash over me. I took a mental picture and sent it deep into my memory bank. This was a moment I never wanted to forget.

26

We had our after-party on New York Street of the back lot. It's a replica of a downtown street, with a bank, a library, a movie theater, and a town square with a big clock in the middle. Of course, there are no backs to the buildings, just posts holding them up, but when you're standing there, it feels like you've been dropped onto main street.

The studio had set up everything for a great party. There was a DJ playing music and long tables filled with every kind of finger food you could want. Shrimp and egg rolls and sushi and mini cheeseburgers and hot chicken wings, and for me, bowls and bowls of guacamole and chips. After the show, the cast had changed into our party clothes. Cassidy looked incredible in her red-leather jacket and boots, and Tyler of course wore the tightest tee shirt he could squeeze into. Martha was all in sequins from head to toe, and for some reason, Ulysses chose to wear his Lincoln stovepipe hat. Luckily, my biological transformation was in good shape, and I had enough energy to become my best Zane Tracy. Tyler even let me borrow his hair products to make my thick human hair look glossy, just like the jar said.

When we climbed out of the mini-van that took us from Stage 42 to the party, everyone cheered. The crew was already there, filling their plates with food. The network executives were huddled in a circle, looking extremely pleased with themselves. Delores must have put on every piece of jewelry she owned, because she glistened like the headlights of a car. You could have used her as a flashlight on a dark, foggy night.

Stan and the other writers of the show were trying their hardest to get into the swing of the party. They're not exactly party folk, as their natural habitat is in front of a computer screen. A couple of them were dancing to the music, searching desperately for the beat. They reminded me of the Supreme Leader when he tried to get his groove on. Even if they were terrible dancers, you loved them for trying.

Sometime after the finger foods but before the hot-fudge sundae bar, Barbara Daniel went to the microphone that had been set up in the town square.

"Everyone," she said. "I have an announcement to make."

It took a while to settle everyone down, but with repeated attempts, she got their attention.

"First of all, I want to congratulate the entire cast and crew of *Oddball Academy* for a very successful season," she began. "This year, we have seen the show flourish and the ratings zoom off the charts. The addition of our new cast member, our resident alien, Buddy Burger, has given us even more reason to celebrate. Cassidy, you had a rough patch this week, but it's so good to see you back to your effervescent self. Your fans have forgiven you and love you."

She paused for everyone to applaud.

"And now for the big announcement. The studio has decided, based on the enthusiastic response to tonight's special, to green-light the *Oddball Academy* movie! Starring Cassidy Cambridge and Buddy Burger, and featuring the entire cast of the show, the movie is scheduled for a Christmas release. We anticipate that it will be a huge hit, and just the beginning of a successful string of movies. I hope you're all ready for the big screen. This is the opportunity of a lifetime, and you earned it!"

The cast and crew broke into wild applause.

"I'm ready for my close-up," Ulysses hollered.

"Your close-up?" Tyler yelled. "What about mine?"

"And my song-and-dance number," Martha yelled.

"And buckets of money," Delores shouted. "Bright, green cash!"

"Buddy," Cassidy said, taking my hands in hers. "We did it. We're going to be movie stars. It's everything we ever dreamed of."

I just smiled at her. This was everything *she* ever dreamed of.

I went to the microphone and whispered in Barbara Daniel's ear.

"Can I say something?" I asked.

"Of course." She stepped aside, and suddenly, I was alone on the stage, facing everyone.

"I would also like to make an announcement," I began. My hands were shaking and so was my voice, but my thoughts were clear. I knew what I wanted to say.

"I am thrilled to hear about the *Oddball Academy* movie, and I know it will be fantastic to make. But, my friends, you are going to have to make it without me."

There was a collective gasp of surprise. I looked over at Barbara Daniel.

"Did you make a deal with another studio?" she said. She looked like she had lost her best friend.

"No," I said. "I would never do that."

"Then why?" she asked.

I took a deep breath and faced the crowd.

"I am not who you think I am," I said. "My real name is Citizen Short Nose, and I am from a red dwarf planet many galaxies away."

"There he goes again," Tyler shouted. "Making up stories. Hogging the spotlight."

"This is my story, and I'm not making it up," I said. "I came to Earth to flee my planet and its repressive government. My grandmother built the spaceship that brought me here. Underneath this human façade is the true alien you have come to know. I was afraid to show him to you. I was afraid you wouldn't accept me the way you have, if you saw the real me."

"Okay, dude. Let's see the real you!" Tyler laughed out loud. "This is going to be good."

Oh, he didn't know how good this was really going to be. I clutched the amulet around my neck.

"Buddy," Cassidy said. "Do you know what you're doing?"

"For the first time in a long time, I really do, Cass."

Holding the amulet in the palm of my hand, I closed my eyes and focused all my energy on my thoughts.

"*Be the real me,*" I chanted to myself. "*Be the real me now.*"

The biological alternation happened quickly. I could feel my human hair receding and my bald, bumpy scalp emerging. As my human skin peeled away, I felt my six eyeballs spring out of my head, replacing the two human ones. My white human teeth disappeared, and my red gums and two tongues took their place.

"What in the world is going on here?" Chuck Smeller said, wiping a sudden burst of sweat from his forehead.

"I always knew aliens were among us," Stan said. "But I didn't know they were actually among *us right here*."

"You mean this guy is an actual extraterrestrial?" Jules, the stage manager, said.

"You bet he is, and he's a pretty cool one," Luis answered.

Meanwhile, my human skin had dissolved all the way down to my knees, freeing my sensory enhancer, which immediately picked up the scent of the mini cheeseburgers. It started to trumpet and shot out toward the food table so hard that it almost carried me with it.

"Whoa," said Ulysses. "That thing really doesn't run on batteries."

"It definitely has a mind of its own," Cassidy said. "Especially when it comes to candy—it's downright dangerous."

"*Be the real me*," I continued to chant, keeping my concentration focused on my transformation. I felt my skin melting all the way down my skinny legs, until my human toes disappeared and my alien suction cups sprang to life with a squishy pop. I opened my eyes, and all I saw was hundreds of eyeballs as big as the moons of Jupiter staring at me.

I heard a loud thud and saw that Delores had hit the ground again, her arms flung out and covered with so much jewelry that she looked like a pirate's treasure chest. Nurse Lisa left Luis's side and rushed over to her.

"She's out cold again," she said. "But I know what to do. Someone bring me water and napkins for her forehead."

"Buddy, I don't believe what I'm seeing," Martha said. "It's like watching special effects in a movie, except it's not a movie."

"You actually grew eyeballs right in front of us," Ulysses said. "That's better than any horror movie I've ever seen. I mean, no offense, on the horror-movie thing."

"Buddy, I . . . I . . . don't know what to say," Barbara Daniel stammered as she gaped at the real me. Chuck Smeller took his handkerchief from his own forehead pocket and put it up to hers, patting her beads of shock sweat away.

"That's enough, Chuck," she snapped. "I can handle my own sweat."

"I say we call the FBI," Tyler said. "They know how to deal with freaks like him."

"That won't be necessary," I said, "because I'm leaving to return to my home planet."

"No, Buddy," Cassidy said. "You didn't tell me that."

"I just made the decision today, Cass."

"But you don't have to leave anymore. The Leader said you could stay here."

"My place isn't here," I said. "There's going to be a revolution taking place on my planet, and I want to be a part of it. I can help my people rediscover themselves. It's what I want to do—and need to do."

"But what about us? Our show? Our movie careers? Our friendship?"

"You will do great with or without me. You have all the talent you need."

"Hey, I'm available for a permanent role," Luis said. "You can't have too many good-looking guys."

"Oh yes you can," Tyler said.

"I wish you'd reconsider, Buddy," Duane said. "I had my doubts about you when I first met you, but you've earned a place in all our hearts."

"And you'll always have a place in mine," I said. "But the universe is calling me, and I have to answer."

"So you're just going to go live out in another galaxy forever?" Martha asked.

"And give up show business?" Ulysses said.

"Maybe he can have his own show on his planet," Martha said.

"I'd like that." I smiled at the thought of it. Maybe Grandma Wrinkle could be my costar.

"Call me if you need a singer," Martha said. "I can sing intergalactically."

"You're certainly loud enough," Ulysses said. "They could probably hear you from Earth."

"Can I help it if I was given the gift of volume?" Martha said.

"Maybe the folks on your planet would enjoy hearing

my rendition of the Gettysburg Address," Ulysses said. "I can do it faster than the speed of light."

I laughed from the inside out. I loved these friends of mine. They were so funny and so accepting. They loved me just as I was, my alien self and all.

"I want to thank all of you for an experience beyond my wildest dreams," I said. "I learned so much from each of you—from you, Ulysses how to laugh; from you, Martha, how to sing from your soul; from you, Tyler, how to style my hair; from you, Duane, how to be a professional; from you, Mary, how to have delicious snacks; and most of all, from you, Luis and Cassidy, how to be a true friend. I'm going to take all your gifts home with me and share them with the citizens of my planet. Even though I'll be light-years away, you'll all be with me every day."

"Buddy," Cassidy said softly. "This sounds like goodbye."

"It's time," I said. I raised my arms and waved to everyone, letting each of my fourteen fingers point to all the different faces in the crowd. "I love you and you and you and you and you and you and you."

I had to fight back tears. If all six of my eyes let loose at once, it would create lavender puddles all over the floor.

"Cassidy and Luis," I said, "why don't you guys walk me to my spaceship."

The sound of applause rang in my ears as we left the party and walked across the back lot to where my spaceship was parked. We passed all the attractions . . . the shark lake, the *Jurassic World* ride, the strawberry ice-cream counter, the pizza parlor, and even the hamburger stand that first gave me the idea for my Earth name, Buddy Cheese Burger. So many memories flooded through my brain, and they were all happy ones.

When we arrived at my spaceship, the three of us stood facing one another, quiet under the Hollywood moon. How could I ever say goodbye to these incredible friends who protected me, stood by me, and loved me no matter what?

"Here, dude," Luis said, handing me a cloth sack with something heavy inside. "It's a bowl of guacamole from Mary. She wanted you to have it for the trip."

"Always thinking of me," I said. "Tell her thank you. And Cassidy, please tell your mom when she wakes up that I can never thank her enough for taking me in and managing my career. And be sure to tell Eloise that she can be anything she wants. She's got the power, and I'll bet she's going to build a great city someday."

Cassidy burst into tears.

"Oh, Buddy, this is so hard," she said. "Will I ever see you again?"

"I hope so. When you look up at the stars and see one twinkling, that's me waving to you."

"What about me, your best dude friend?" Luis said. "I don't get a wave?"

"I'll get Citizen Cruel to send you an intergalactic squawk."

"On second thought, don't bother. I'll borrow Cassidy's twinkle."

We all laughed, a bittersweet laugh, knowing it was our last laugh together on Earth. We threw our arms around one another and hugged until we couldn't hug any more.

Then I turned and walked up the ladder, opened the hatch, and climbed into my ship.

I set the trajectory for home. As the ship blasted off, I looked out the window and saw Cassidy and Luis growing smaller and smaller, waving until they were just dots on the spinning blue Earth below me. I settled into my seat and felt the surge of speed as I headed past Mars and the moons of Jupiter toward the little red planet I called home. My grandmother would be waiting for me, along with a whole new world of freedom.

I reached over to the cloth sack and took out the bowl of guacamole. Picking up one of the chips, I dipped it into the bowl and popped the whole thing into my mouth.

It was really good.

ACKNOWLEDGMENTS

We deeply appreciate the efforts of everyone at Abrams Kids, especially Andrew Smith, who said yes to bringing Buddy Burger to life, and our editor, Maggie Lehrman, whose deft judgment helped shape Buddy's intergalactic adventures. Many thanks to Hallie Patterson, Mary Marolla, and Jenny Choy who have been so instrumental in introducing the world to our favorite Alien Superstar. They are superstars in their own right!

Ethan Nicolle's humorous art brings our characters to life with great style and adds immeasurably to our reader's experience. We thank him for his talent and commitment.

Our agents, Esther Newberg and Ellen Goldsmith-Vein, have been constant champions of our vision and make it possible for our imaginations to flourish. Mostly, we are grateful for our almost twenty-year collaboration, which has resulted in a body of work that we are both proud of. This is our thirty-sixth novel together, and we are hopeful that we can continue to entertain our young readers and warm their hearts and minds.

Henry Winkler and Lin Oliver
Hollywood, 2021